DEADLY GREEN

An antiques' raid goes wrong in rural Kent, and a man dies. In the desperate cover-up that follows, it becomes suddenly all too easy to have a fatal accident. Few in the little village of Otley Ash are spared a share of terror: not Old Esther, half gipsy and wholly eccentric; not Violet, the resident busybody; not the Channings on their farm among the oast houses, nor the Reads working the recently restored windmill. For somewhere out there is a killer . . .

Books by Evelyn Harris
in the Linford Mystery Library:

DOWN AMONG THE DEAD MEN
MEDIUM FOR MURDER

EVELYN HARRIS

DEADLY GREEN

Complete and Unabridged

LINFORD
Leicester

First published in Great Britain in 1981 by
Robert Hale Limited
London

First Linford Edition
published 2001
by arrangement with
Robert Hale Limited
London

British Library CIP Data

Harris, Evelyn
    Deadly green.—Large print ed.—
Linford mystery library
    1. Detective and mystery stories
    2. Large type books
    I. Title
    823.9′14 [F]

ISBN 0–7089–9730–9

Published by
F. A. Thorpe (Publishing)
Anstey, Leicestershire

Set by Words & Graphics Ltd.
Anstey, Leicestershire
Printed and bound in Great Britain by
T. J. International Ltd., Padstow, Cornwall

This book is printed on acid-free paper

1

A worm lay beside his hand; a worm of blood, washed into pinkness by the morning dew. Rolfe stared at it with dulled eyes. His worm: his blood. But surely he must have stopped bleeding now? Too quickly, he moved his head, and the pain slammed him flat.

Retching, he remained pressed, face downwards, to the bottom of the overgrown ditch where he had spent the last few hours. How many hours? He had no idea. And no means of finding out. His watch, too, had been ripped from his wrist, along with most of the flesh from his lower arm. But it was morning, at least that much was certain; very early morning, with the September dew still thick on the leaves and the spiders' webs grey with moisture in the drenched grasses. So he had obviously made it through the terrible night.

He moved again, groaning in spite of

himself. His swollen tongue came out from between his teeth, roving questingly against the wet herbage. He knew his injuries were severe, the dogs had bitten to the bone. Trained to kill, they had gone for his throat and savaged when deflected from their aim. Mercifully, he could not see himself and hardly realised that half his face had been torn away. Now and again, his straying fingers would feel momentarily for cheek or chin or lip, hovering over the blood-crusted flesh as if it belonged to somebody else. But numbness first, and then unconsciousness, had blocked suffering. Now, it seemed, the respite had ended; with renewed senses came pain. Rolfe thrust it aside.

Hauling himself to a sitting position, he leaned back against the slope of the ditch and looked around him. Everywhere appeared peaceful enough. In all the wide landscape of hills and woods and fields, the only living creatures seemed to be the round, white sheep which dotted the downland. But country people rose early and he had no intention of being caught out in the open by some farm-worker, or child gathering mushrooms. Yet it was necessary to travel by daylight; yesterday he had holed up until evening, but he dared not risk another night's exposure. If he kept to the hedgerows and ditches, and the woodland where there was plenty of cover, he should be safe enough. He calculated that he must have another three or four miles to go, and tried to visualise the map again. Having been in the area but once before, he found the surrounding terrain offered no clue to his whereabouts; he would have to find the village and take his bearings from there.

Before he had keeled over, hurt and weakened as he was, he had already managed to cross the white scar of the new motorway, which was carving a relentless groove through the chalk of the gentle downs; and he had waded the river Addot, broad and shallow below its sluice, not once but several times, as it looped the fields along the valley. The night had also seen him across pastures and cornfields, dark woodlands and slopes of rabbit-bitten turf, each stumbled over with all he had left of strength, and that driving will which had forced his shaking, shock-deadened body to keep going, spurring him to place one slow foot in front of the other, step after step, when all he wanted to do was sleep, till his mind was blind and he was no longer conscious of wanting even that. But, somehow, he had kept on the move. Until Nature herself had sent him out like a snuffed candle.

His fingers tightened convulsively on the soaking grass beside him. The slight movement disturbed a robin which belled a warning and dipped away across his sight, gay as a blown russet leaf, sunlight on its breast. Around him, hedges smoked upwards in the sun. Somewhere, a long way off, an earth-mover rumbled into action. Painfully, Rolfe dragged himself to his feet, clinging to a stripling oak that thrust from the ditch. A shower of water-drops splattered across his shoulders. His limbs felt stiff and heavy, as if encased in lead, and, for a few moments, refused to obey his will. Then his arms and legs propelled his body forward and

4

he found himself standing in full sunshine on a rutted cart-track which wound away towards a thick belt of trees on his left. Walking like an old man, he headed for its shelter.

What he was about to do now was against all orders. If anything went wrong, they had been told, each man was on his own. No one stayed to help another; no one contacted anyone else; they got out, and got out fast, and waited for further instructions. And, if caught, they kept their mouths shut. Certainly, thought Rolfe sourly, no one had waited to give him a hand when he found himself in difficulties. His prudent mates had melted away like snow in summer at the first hint of trouble. But there was to have been no trouble, was there? So what went wrong?

The raid had been planned meticulously. They had been made to memorise the plan of the house, the alarm systems, the servants' habits and their quarters; and each had been drilled thoroughly in his own particular part in the robbery — drilled and drilled again until they were sick of the sight and sound of Kenlake House and everything in it. There wasn't one of them who didn't know the life-history and present customs of Adnan Al Begrar, and his princess, better than they knew their own. But one couldn't lift a fortune without expending a little sweat and blood . . .

And they had so nearly pulled the whole thing off. The bulk of the most valuable stuff had already been loaded when he, Rolfe, had tangled with those three Dobermann pinschers. He gave a grimace. Diabolical, that. The dogs had been his province. The dogs and their handlers. And he had put the lot out of action, or so he had thought. What he had not known, what nobody appeared to have known, was that the princess had not left that morning as planned. Whoever had occupied the large black limousine, it had not been her. And she had retained her own four-legged body-guard.

Almost in slow motion, he reran within his head that last scene in Kenlake House. He, alone in the princess's bedroom, with the small second jewel-safe already open; she, standing by the door, one slender hand on the leash that held the dogs. For a split second their eyes had met and he had thought, as she slipped the leash: She bloody well means to kill me! Even now, that shock churned his gut anew. Quite deliberately, she had sent the dogs in, not to hold, but to tear out his throat. And, almost, they had succeeded. He still could not fathom how he had managed to escape. The slavering jaws, the rending teeth, the terrible screaming — his own screams, he realised now, torn from his mangled mouth — were all part of that hideous nightmare, a blur that forbade total recall. Yet, somehow, he must have given a vicious account of himself. His own gun had dispatched one dog, before being torn from his fingers and skittering across the carpet; another of his attackers had fallen, dying, at his feet, its skull crushed by the only thing he could grab to hand — a heavy, golden, flame-shaped object. And, all the while, like a slim, golden flame herself, the princess had stood there, watching. May she rot in hell!

Rolfe felt the sweat start on his forehead. But he had something of hers to remember her by. By God he had! His fingers closed around the smooth coldness in his pocket. They were his way out of this mess. 'If anything goes wrong, you are on your own,' the Boss had said. Well — not if he, Rolfe, could help it, he wasn't; he was going to be crow-bait if he didn't get assistance soon. So he was going to the top. The Boss would hardly pass up a sure million.

Within the wood it was cool and shadowed, and dank with the smell of earth and rotting leaves. If he avoided the heavier undergrowth, mainly blackberry bushes and stands of honeysuckle and wild clematis, Rolfe found the going easy enough and he lurched forward at a reasonable pace — or what would have been a reasonable pace for a crippled cow, he thought bitterly, twenty minutes later, pausing for breath and clutching for support at the branch of a twisted yew.

Oak and ash and birch grew thickly together, with here and there one of the darker, more ancient yews, but it did not appear to be the kind of wood where children played. The only sign that something human had ever set foot in that place was a tall, rusting water-tower, which reared its head between the trees like an enormous spider; a relic from some wartime army camp, if the over-grown concrete foundations scattered around were anything to go by. That they were there he found out by the simple process of tripping over one and falling flat on his face, jarring his body on the cruel hidden stonework. The pain, which had become a dull, constant rack, bearable, like a bad toothache, suddenly flared up once more into full-blast hellfire. Rolfe sat, gasping.

It was very quiet under the densely-leafed trees. No birds. No animals. No insects that he could see. Only the sound of his ragged, hurtful breathing. For the first time it occurred to him that perhaps he wasn't going to come out of this, after all; that perhaps the dogs had done a better job than he had realised, or that he, himself, was swiftly finishing their butchery. He dragged his protesting body up and stood, swaying. For a minute he wondered if he could climb the water-tower, hide there. Then common sense came back to him. For one thing, he would never make it to the top: the rotting ladder-rungs finished a good twelve feet above his head and he had not the strength left for girder-climbing; for another, he needed medical help, warmth, comfort, food. There was only one chance for him, one place to go. And he was going. He had no intention of being the only one to founder with the bloody ship. Teeth set against the hurt, he pushed himself on his way again.

When he emerged from the trees on to the open downland, the sun was well up, a layer of living gold across the harvest-fields below him. A combine harvester, small as a toy in the distance, was whirring away down on his left, turning the great meadow where it worked into honeyed bands of light and shade. There was the smell of wild thyme, and warm chalk, and something deeper, more pungent, which increased steadily in potency as he headed downhill, keeping to the cover of the dogwood bushes until he reached the hedgerow. Beyond, lay a field of stubble, its edges laced with early September's harvest weeds, vetches and pimpernels and corn chamomile, fierce fire-bursts of poppies and the plant-strangling, sweet-scented bindweed. Tugging a hobbling length of pink-and-white flowers from around one of his canvas boots, he slouched his slow path forward over the bristling acres. A narrow lane twisted its way on the other side of the far hedge, but, though passage would have been easier there, Rolfe dared not take the risk of being seen and continued to hug the inner side of the hedgerow.

The pungent smell had become noticeably stronger, reminding him irresistibly of cool beer, and breweries, and suddenly he realised that the tang in his nostrils came from the ripe hops in the hopfields which lined the other side of the lane. A few paces further, and the oast-houses themselves came into view, three circular brick-built kilns for drying the hops, each with a conical roof and white-painted wooden ventilation cowl cocked for the wind. Rolfe paused to listen. Above his own rapid, harsh breathing he could hear, faintly, the sound of a tractor, and voices from a distance, carried on the breeze. He guessed that the farmhouse itself must be somewhere near by.

Knowing that he was too close to civilisation for safety, he determined to strike off at an angle across the corner of the field. But first he risked a glance at the signpost in the lane. Otley Ash. His breath went out in a painful rasp of relief. He knew where he was now and a few minutes' walking confirmed his judgement. The church spire was thrusting up through the trees, a slender column, ornately decorated, like the tiers of a wedding-cake. His goal lay on the further side — and uphill.

A groan ripped from his throat. He would never manage the distance, certainly not over rough terrain, his legs were already buckling beneath him. Perhaps, if he rested . . . He collapsed heavily to the ground, his mouth hanging open in a black, crusted gape. The village would have to be skirted, that much was plain. He tried to visualise its structure: the church and then the rectory, a row of cottages — no, a small orchard and then the row of cottages . . . Or was there a pond? Somewhere there, he was sure, he had seen a pond. He did not seem able to think straight; there was a buzzing in his head and his eyes would not focus. Wearily he closed his lids. Suppose he were to steal a car? But from where? He could hardly drag his way along the main street of the village in his present condition. Besides, surely the police must already have been alerted and have their eyes on all the outlying villages? God, if he could only think clearly. So many questions and no answers.

The buzzing in his head increased and he opened his eyes again to find the sound was not entirely in his imagination. He was surrounded by wasps. He was sitting in the long grass at the edge of a plum orchard. The plums, purple-black and ripe, hung thickly on the branches and a great many had fallen and were rotting on the ground. It was among these that the wasps were crawling. Hastily Rolfe removed himself from their vicinity and discovered he was once more standing on a grass track, one which circled the rear of the churchyard. It seemed as good a way to go as any, there being a ditch close by the churchyard wall that would provide cover if necessary, and he limped along it, his body bent in a complaining curve.

Once he heard voices from the other side of the wall, childish trebles, high and quarrelsome, then a man's voice, speaking in soft placation. Once, too, the sound of a horse nearby, its hooves striking a sharp tattoo along the lane. And laughter, floating on the polished air. The clang of a gate. But nothing to alarm him unduly.

He had nearly reached the end of the churchyard wall when a large brown dog came bounding towards him. Rolfe froze in fear, then pulled himself together, guessing that where there was a dog there was probably an owner, following. He went into the ditch among the hogweed and brambles like a jack-rabbit and crouched close under a spreading elder, his hunted eyes straining through the spinning light between the leaves. The dog bounded after him, waving its tail frantically and emitting slobbering little grunts of pleasure.

'Go home, you brute,' hissed Rolfe savagely, hitting it hard across the muzzle. The animal quivered in reproach, but stood its ground. A piercing whistle made it turn its head, but its feet remained four-square firm. Then it swung its nose to Rolfe again, whining. Rolfe held his breath. A man's voice gave a sharp command and the dog went, reluctantly, with a last slavering shake of its jaw, to bounce at its master's heel.

Rolfe wiped the sweat and spittle out of his eyes, silently blessing the elder-tree with its predilection for the dead. That shave had been too close for comfort. However, he reached the far end of the village without mishap and crossed the lane at a convenient bend, shuffling his way along the edge of a beanfield on the other side, with his arm wrapped around his body in an attempt to hold himself together. Twice he fell and twice he staggered to his feet and carried on, each punishing step punctuated by a ragged gasp.

The buzzing had returned to his ears and he had started to bleed again, he wasn't sure from where; the puncture wound in his thigh, he thought, or it could have been his arm. He tried to lift the latter to examine it; tried to focus his dimming gaze, but neither the muscles of his arm, nor the balls of his eyes, would obey his wishes. For several heartbeats the heavens reeled in sympathetic semi-circles and Rolfe found himself retching, his empty stomach twisting itself upwards into his mouth. Then he fell and this time he did not rise. He was still conscious. He could hear water, falling softly in a spray, and the ground beside him was damp, the bottom of the ditch there running in a tiny, weed-choked river, and he could see toadflax flattened beneath him, its bearded yellow-and-orange flowers already stained with spreading red.

Branches shifted and rustled overhead, netting him in shadow. Tall oaks and a silver birch. Further along, a group of hazels offered more protection, their leaves a green-gold screen above the bleaching herbage. Grasping a tussock of grass, Rolfe heaved himself forward a few painful paces before again collapsing, half hunched, the uninjured side of his face resting on his sound arm and the agonised breath bubbling in his chest. He fought desperately to stay conscious. 'Keep your mouth shut,' the Boss had said, 'whatever happens. I'll take care of you.' They had had their orders: no contact. Easy enough, then, to agree. But who ever expected disaster? Rolfe coughed hurtfully. And could he really trust anyone to pluck him from the arms of the police, once they held him? He did not think so.

He pulled himself forward again and lay on his side in the shelter of the hazel boughs. Well, the Boss was going to take care of him all right and he, Rolfe, was going to be on hand to make sure that he did. He reached for his insurance and held it gloatingly in his palm. Two enormous emeralds, square-cut and perfectly matched, blinking at him with deadly green eyes. Worth a queen's ransom, so it was said. Sheba's Barter. Yes, worth a cool million in anyone's book: Adnan Al Begrar would give that to recover them for his princess.

At that moment Rolfe heard, not far away, the crunch of dry leaves underfoot and steps treading the grass towards him. He shrank into the shadows. Waited . . . It was all right; the figure was moving past, would have gone — but Rolfe gave a sudden hoarse shout and struggled from his hiding-place. Help had come. He had not been abandoned: they had come for him, after all — the Boss would see that he was fixed up. His bubbling cry brought the other round in a sharp twist and, after a second's hesitation, the feet retraced their path to stand beside the wounded man. Rolfe peered upwards. The sun hurt his eyes and he could see his rescuer only as a black blur against the light.

'Rolfe — ?'

'Am I glad to see you!' Rolfe husked out on a sobbing breath. His fingers groped across the shoe beside him, found an ankle and grasped it, straining to pull himself upright. With no help forthcoming he was unable to manage the feat and pitched forward in a shuddering huddle. A shaft of light, slanting down through the hazel branches, sent his companion's shadow swooping like a bat across the grass.

'What happened?' The voice came at last, cold as the winter wind.

'Didn't the others tell you?' Rolfe bubbled painfully. Surely, by now, the main haul from Kenlake House must have been safely at its destination?

'I'd still like your version.'

With frequent pauses, Rolfe's ruined mouth fought to frame an intelligible and quick account of the last twenty-four hours.

'And that was all?'

Wasn't it enough? thought Rolfe resentfully. They had brought out a fortune between them. But he still had his trump card. His insurance.

'Don't forget the emeralds,' he said.

'Oh, by all means let's not forget the emeralds!'

Rolfe held out the stones, their green

fire burning malevolently, streaked in blood.

The pale blur of face above him swam down to his level and he was able to see the eyes clearly for the first time, narrowed now and as pitiless as a preying bird's. And Rolfe knew that he had made his final mistake.

2

Lucy Channing cantered down the ride. Sixteen, ash-blonde, and very pretty, she sat her horse with an assurance that bordered on arrogance. Along the ride, under the dipping branches, out on to the sunny grass track that led to Channings' Farm, through the plum orchard, with a wave to the fruit-pickers, past the barns and outbuildings, and she was dismounting in the yard in front of the beautiful old farmhouse. Her boots crunched the loose golden gravel.

'Shall I see to your horse, Miss Lucy?' asked an ingratiating voice at her elbow. Lucy turned, frowning. Reuben Colley had oozed from nowhere, as usual.

'No, thank you,' she said curtly. 'I'll attend to him myself. I'm sure you must have other things to do.'

'Your Ma wants you. Looking for you for more'n ten minutes, she was.'

Lucy hesitated, flinging a wary glance

towards the house.

'Important, she said,' went on Reuben.

Reluctantly Lucy handed him the reins and watched him walk away, leading the horse behind him. She disliked Reuben Colley; she disliked both the Colley brothers. She disliked their sly black eyes and their oily grins and the habit they had of sidling up on people unawares. And, most of all, she disliked that obsequious manner which hid a total dedication to their own ends. If it had been up to her, she would have sent them packing long ago, but her father and her brother, Tom, considered the Colleys to be useful and hard-working.

Reuben and Jordan had been a part of the scheme of things at Channings' Farm for as long as Lucy could remember. They were all that was left of the gipsy families which used to come each year to the farm for the hop-picking. Then, the hop-bines had all been stripped by hand, a task needing a vast army of workers, migrants mostly, who came for the seasonal three weeks in September and were housed in huts on spare ground beside the orchard.

A row of those huts still stood, mouldering, their window-frames rotted, the corrugated iron roofs rusting into holes, as much relics of a time gone as the concrete gun-emplacements that still dotted the countryside.

Today the few casual workers lived in smart caravans, while the hops were picked by an enormous machine, located in a shed behind the barn. The iron monster required only a handful of acolytes to feed it bines and dance attendance. But Reuben and Jordan continued to arrive each year as regularly as clockwork, to help with the harvest and to see the hops safely in and dried. What they did, or where they went, for the rest of the year was their own secret; there were rumours that they dismembered old cars in a yard outside Adford. Certainly Reuben especially had a knack with machinery that took some of the summertime burden off Tom's shoulders.

Lucy wrenched open the door of the farmhouse and slammed it behind her.

'Is that you, Lucy?' A small woman with Lucy's clear-cut features and a fading fair prettiness stepped into the hall. 'You've just missed the rector.'

'That's good,' said Lucy.

'He wants you to — '

'No!' said Lucy, swinging into the sunny kitchen where the rest of her family had been drinking coffee. Her brother looked up with a faint smile.

'Let me finish,' protested Marjorie Channing, removing an empty cup from the table at her husband's elbow and carefully skirting the stool on which his heavily bandaged foot was resting. He had had a disturbed night and had fallen asleep in the winged chair.

Lucy tossed her jacket on a peg. 'Whatever it is, the answer is still no.'

Tom and Beth Channing exchanged amused glances. From long experience, they knew their gentle mother needed no ally. She was as water, constant dripping on a stone.

'He wants you to play the organ,' grinned Tom.

'You must be joking!' Lucy's indignant voice climbed the scale.

'Sssh! You'll waken your father,' said

Marjorie Channing. 'Miss Amory's broken her wrist; she can hardly play for the church festival concert with her arm in plaster.'

'I doubt if anyone would notice the difference,' drawled Tom lazily, winking up at his sister, Beth, who was perched on the arm of his chair.

'Tom!' Marjorie turned back to her youngest daughter. 'Mr Waterhouse has worked so hard to make the whole thing a success. How can you refuse, Lucy?'

'Very easily,' said Lucy hardily. 'Watch me.'

'It's in aid of the church heating fund.'

'It can be in aid of his new bedsocks, for all I care. I'm already singing a solo,' said Lucy. 'That's my contribution to the evening. Why can't Beth play the organ?' She scowled across at her sister.

'He doesn't want Beth,' said Marjorie, making her eldest daughter's name sound like an attack of death-watch beetle. Whatever musical ability the Channing family possessed, it was seen as being centred firmly in Lucy.

'Very lucky for her,' said Lucy sourly.

Beth spread her hands and gave a wry lift to one shoulder.

'There's the choir to rehearse, too,' went on Marjorie. 'You can't let him down, Lucy, he's a good, kind man.'

Lucy snorted. 'Why couldn't we have a hunting, shooting, fishing rector, like the one at Connington, rather than a blessed, holy saint?'

'Said parson of Connington drinks like a drain,' remarked Tom, his mouth curled on the edge of laughter.

'So will I, at this rate.' Lucy poured herself a cup of coffee. 'Have you heard that choir?'

'Every Sunday,' said Marjorie. 'Anyhow, you've put them through their paces before.'

'Which is why I don't intend to stick my neck out again. That ghastly Georgie Mumford is in it.'

'Everyone will be going to the festival,' said Marjorie.

Her husband stirred in his chair. 'I won't.'

Marjorie turned to him. 'Oh, you're

awake, T.J. Do you want another cup of coffee?'

He shook his head. 'Isn't this concert where Ingham's diva is going to sing?'

'That's right.'

'Then what does it matter who plays the damned organ? She'll think we're a lot of hicks, anyhow.' He moved his foot cautiously on the stool. 'How did old Ingham persuade the woman to bring her talents down here?'

Marjorie replied: 'Evidently he was at school with her. You know Ingham Read: he socialises with most people of note in the area.'

'And everyone likely to do him any good,' said T.J. He spotted Tom for the first time and sat up sharply in his chair and roared: 'What's damned Tom doing in here? Why isn't he out with the hop-picking machine? It's broken down again, hasn't it?'

'I've been working on it all morning,' said Tom sullenly.

'Bloody hell — '

'He's only come in for a cup of coffee,' soothed Marjorie.

27

'I tell you what,' broke in Lucy, eyes narrowed to slits of calculation. 'I'll do a deal.'

'A deal?' echoed Marjorie faintly.

'Yes. I'll play the organ for the concert, and in church on Sunday, and I'll drill the choir — if you let me go to the Reads' party.'

Big Tom Channing, known to all simply as T.J., looked at his youngest daughter with approval. The baby of the family, nine years younger than Beth, ten years younger than Tom, she knew how to handle her mother; she knew how to handle him, come to that. He beamed at her fondly. The child most like him in temperament, it was a constant disappointment to him that she was not the first-born of the family; she could run rings around the other two. Lucy knew where she was going: Beth and Tom wouldn't even recognise it when they got there. He growled: 'That's my girl.'

Marjorie, more cautious, said: 'What kind of party?'

'Just a party. At the Reads' place. Everyone is going. I met Archer Read in the village this morning and he invited me. I was wondering how I could put it to you, because everybody acts so oddly these days whenever his name is mentioned. He used virtually to live here and now — pouf! — he never comes near. I know Beth and Tom quarrelled with him, but I didn't, and I don't see why — '

'I didn't quarrel with him,' said Marjorie. 'And he never comes near me, either.'

'I expect he's busy at the windmill,' said T.J. 'He's worked the place up into a thriving concern, not merely a tourist attraction with a bit of flour for the village thrown in as a bonus — but as a paying enterprise. Ingham says they've pulled some big outside orders, with the prospect of more to come. Ingham Read always did fall on his feet.'

'It's Archer who does the work,' said Marjorie.

'But it is Ingham's business sense. He's lucky in his son. Damned Tom won't do an ounce more than necessary.'

'So I can go?' Lucy looked at her mother.

'Well, I don't know — ' began Marjorie, her eyes on the faces of her two eldest children. Beth looked distressed; Tom, angry.

'You can't let her go!' burst out Tom. 'You know the stories that are circulating in the village.'

'You would say that,' said Lucy, eyes flashing blue sparks, 'just because you and Beth had some kind of tiff with him. But I like Archer. At least he knows what he wants from life.'

'Oh, he'd know that,' said Tom.

'You used to be friends.'

Rivals, thought Marjorie. Tom and Archer were the same age, Beth a year younger, and, though they had always been together, even in childhood it had been an uneasy three-cornered partnership.

'Anyhow, I don't see what it's got to do with damned Tom,' roared T.J. 'I make the decisions in this house and, if I say Lucy can go to Reads' place, then she can go. Archer's not a bad lad.'

'You haven't seen him in months,' said Tom quietly.

30

'He's not likely to have grown two heads and a tail. And he works a damned sight harder than you, from all accounts.'

Marjorie Channing watched silently, waiting for her two eldest children to close ranks, as they always did at the first sign of trouble.

True to form, Beth paddled in her oar. 'That would be difficult. Tom's been up at four and not in bed till after midnight these past few weeks.'

T.J. rounded on her. 'Then what does he bloody well do with his time, eh? Tell me that. Nothing useful, that's for sure. He should be out there now getting that bloody hop-picking machine moving.'

'Blast the bloody hop-picking machine,' muttered Tom.

'What?' T.J.'s neck swelled redly, but before he could burst out further Lucy's arm went around his neck.

'Then I may go to Archer's on Thursday?' she wheedled. 'Please.'

T.J. squeezed her hand. This was the only one of the family who did not rile him unbearably. 'Yes,' he said. 'If it's all right with your mother.'

'With respect,' said Tom, not looking at all respectful, 'I don't think you realise what Archer's like these days. It's months since you had anything to do with him. He's changed.'

'I heard he'd become a bit wild,' ventured Marjorie.

'Oh, you know what this village is like,' said Lucy impatiently. 'One slip and one's branded as a raving sex-fiend.'

'So — ' roared T.J. 'If Beth gives him the elbow he's not going to sit at home moping, is he? What do you expect? She had her chance and she blew it. And now she's taken up with this other fellow — this what's-his-name — who's not even a local lad. Best farm in the district, the Reads', and she threw it over because of some silly squabble.'

'Beth's known Archer all her life,' said Marjorie gently. 'After his mother died he spent most of his waking hours here.' Ingham had had little time for children and none for his eldest son. 'The boy was more like a brother than a lover. You can't blame her if she wants a bit more romance.'

T.J. snorted. 'Perhaps you should have told him to clout her over the head with a carnation.'

'Little Archie Read,' mused Marjorie. 'Do you remember when — ?'

'He's big Archie Read, now,' said Tom, 'with an eye to the main chance, like his father.'

'You can't fault him for that,' said Lucy. 'I'd be the same.' She smiled down at her father and kissed the top of his head. 'I know Ingham's a bit of an old rake, but there's nothing wrong with Archer. What say I keep him in the family?'

'He's much too old for you,' protested Marjorie. 'You're only sixteen.' She made it sound like a disease.

Lucy laughed. 'But I'll recover from that.' She gave a wicked grin. 'I'm up for bids.'

'Lucy!' Her mother frowned.

'She's only trying to provoke you,' said Beth. 'She's not as hard-headed as she likes to pretend.'

'A little hard-headedness is what we need in this family,' snarled T.J. 'Perhaps you and Tom should try it some time.' He stared across at Beth, where she sat on the arm of Tom's chair. Pretty enough, he'd grant her that. Not a beauty like Lucy, of course, but pretty enough. He studied his eldest children, the two dark heads shot with gold from the sun. Healthy bodies, smooth, tanned skin, strong white teeth and good shoulders. They were a good-looking family. He himself had been a handsome man in his youth. He smiled slightly, remembering. And with a dash of the devil along with it. Lucy had a dash of the devil in her, too — and she would never put up with anything that was not to her taste . . . It was a pity Tom didn't possess a few of her guts. He looked at his son with dislike. Oh, the boy had a temper when goaded long enough, but it needed a whole heap of prodding to get him going. Mild as milk, most of the time. And it didn't do. Not if one were to be the boss, it didn't do. People took advantage.

With a start, he realised that Beth was regarding him steadily, holding his eyes with her own, and he had an uncomfortable feeling that she knew what he was thinking. Both she and Tom had their mother's eyes. Deep grey and clear, and fringed with dark lashes. Nice eyes. But not Channing eyes. Channing eyes were a fierce blue like his own. Like his father's eyes and his grandfather's before him. Like Lucy's, which looked out on the world with a straight, fearless gaze.

The farm had been in the Channing family for generations, as Ingham Read's had been in his, and the Deauvilles' and the Suttons' and the Brownings' had been in theirs. Proud old families that had farmed the same land for centuries. Things were changing, though. It was becoming harder and harder to hold on to what one had. Of course, some people managed all right. Like Ingham Read and his son, Archer. T.J. turned to his own son. 'Isn't it time you got back to work?'

'I'm going. I'm going.' Tom rose to his feet.

'You did damn all yesterday afternoon.'

'That was hardly my fault.' Tom's voice was cold. 'I had the police here making enquiries about that man found dead near Rudd's smallholding and they wanted to interview the work force, find out if anyone had seen anything. I had to go round with them, as you very well know.'

'Of course you did,' said T.J. sarcastically. 'Much easier than putting in a few hours' solid work, wasn't it?'

Tom's eyes darkened and Marjorie said hurriedly: 'Did you hear any more about yesterday's affair in the village this morning, Lucy? Poor Esther. It must have been a terrible shock for her, finding that man dead in the ditch; they say he was torn to pieces.'

'The police are still around, asking questions, but no one seems to have seen anything and I don't suppose they'd admit to it if they had. I was talking to the local reporter outside the Bell and he says the man was someone called Rolfe, who belonged to a gang posing as workmen that robbed Kenlake House the previous day. They got away with millions of pounds of stuff — '

'That's an exaggeration, surely?'

'He said not. Jewellery and antiques

36

and such. You know what these rich Arabs are like.'

'Serves them right for locking the place up,' said T.J. 'We never had the gates closed on us before and no one stole anything then, and people were in and out all the time. Kept open house, the Kenlakes did.'

Marjorie turned to her eldest daughter. 'Beth, I think you should go up and see if Esther is all right. She wants some more straw for her corn dollies, anyway.'

'Mother means pump her,' laughed Lucy. 'Find out all about the crime on our doorstep from the horse's mouth. The whole village is agog. We've never had anything like this before.'

Marjorie disagreed. 'There was young Carl Ray, a couple of years ago.'

'I don't count him,' said Lucy. 'He shot himself rather than stand trial, after the police found out he'd assaulted that little girl.'

'Silly young fool,' commented T.J.

'I don't know,' said Tom. 'It was probably better for his family that way.' He put his hand on the door. 'If he'd gone to prison, their lives would have been hell.'

'I think perhaps they were,' said Marjorie quietly. 'Did you know that Ingham Read has bought them out?'

'Yes, I heard. He's after Esther Deauville's place, too.'

'Well, Esther will never sell Elderwood.'

'He'll scoop it soon enough when she snuffs it,' said T.J. 'And for a song, I'll be bound, as it's falling down about her ears.'

His wife raised her eyebrows. 'Old Esther's good for a few more years yet; she's strong as an ox.'

'She'd enjoy hearing you say that,' said Beth. 'I'd better run the straw up to her now, before I start on the books. I suppose she wants wheat-straw — and all cut neatly by hand?' Her tone was resigned. 'I'll take the Land-Rover.'

'I'll come with you,' said Tom.

'No, you will not,' said his father. 'You'll go and help Reuben with the hop-picking machine.'

'There's also Esther's poultry feed,' put in Marjorie, stacking cups in the sink.

'That might as well go up there, too. Esther may need it. And it's heavy for Beth to handle.'

'Tom can load it then,' said T.J. grudgingly.

'And who is to shift it the other end?' asked Beth, her voice smooth as silk. 'Me and old Esther?'

T.J. cursed roundly. 'Take it, then, Tom, damn you, and get back here as fast as you can.' He winced as he moved in his chair. 'If this bloody foot wasn't on me, I'd show you a thing or two.'

'Perhaps if you'd improve your bloody temper, you'd improve your bloody foot as well,' bit out Tom softly between his teeth.

'Don't you bloody well swear at me, young Tom.'

'I don't see why not; you do it to me — all the time.'

'Now, now, now,' chided Marjorie, flapping a tea-towel.

'Oh, for God's sake — Come on, Beth,' rapped Tom. 'I can't stand it in here a minute longer. Let's load the stuff for Esther.'

'And then get back here and do some work,' shouted his father after him.

'Work? I never stop,' grumbled Tom, as he and Beth stepped into the sunshine. 'I think I must have been born with an Irish teaspoon. And nothing I do suits the old man. He considers I'm some sort of lackey. When it pleases him he sends me here, sends me there, like some errand boy. And still he's never satisfied. I can't be in two places at once. He keeps on about that damned hop-picking machine. If he'd leave me alone, I'd get on with the job, but he won't. It's 'go here, do that . . . ' from morning till night, and I've just about had it up to my crop. I'm telling you, Beth, I'll not stand much more of it.'

'He's in pain,' said Beth. 'He'll be better later on.'

'Will he? I wonder. I think he has it in for me for ever,' replied Tom bitterly. 'Do you hear how he refers to me, so regularly that he doesn't even realise he's doing it? 'Damned Tom'.

'If I could just see an end . . . ' He lifted a sack of grain into the back of the

Land-Rover. 'If I were to go — would you come with me, Beth?'

'Where? To do what? Besides, you can't leave him, Tom. He needs you.'

'Like hell, he does. He needs a whipping-boy, that's all. Any one of the men could do for him what I do. Reuben's good with the machinery, anyhow. And there's Paul Pace — '

'The other men won't work for Reuben.'

'He should have thought of that sooner . . . ' Tom strode round the Land-Rover. 'We'll just collect Esther's straw and then we'll be on our way. What is it she wants? Wheat from the experimental field?'

Beth nodded. 'That's the strongest.' She followed her brother across the gravel and round behind the barn, where pheasants were tamely pecking grain on a piece of waste land. As they turned alongside the large shed which housed the hop-picking machine, Reuben Colley materialised from within.

'Almost ready to go now, Mister Tom,' he said.

41

'Right, Reuben. Just check that everything's working, then round up the lads from the lower hopfield; they've started picking there by hand. Everyone knows what to do. I'll have a word with the women myself. They went to the bean-field this morning, but I can bring a couple back to help sort over the hops. I won't be long. About an hour.' He cast a glance at the oast-houses. 'When I get back we'll fire the burner. Under number three oast, I think, to start with. I know she's a bit temperamental, but I want to keep her going. Have you raked the dried hops from number two?'

'Yes, Mister Tom. They're all ready to be bagged.'

'Good. Get someone on the press. Once the picking-machine moves into its stride we should soon catch up on our backlog.' He turned his head. 'Where's Jordan?'

'Down there.' Reuben jerked his head in the direction of the nearest hopfield. 'The guv'nor told him to cut down those bushes and nettles beside the gate.'

'Damn! When was he told that?'

'Yesterday afternoon, when you went off with that policeman.'

'All right. He's probably almost finished by now. I'll get him back for you and you can put him on the press.' Tom swung away along the track that led past the oasts.

'One of the bolt-plates has split on the elevator belt,' called Reuben after him. 'I've rigged up a temporary replacement, but it won't last long.'

Tom glanced up at the elevator which transported the sacks of freshly-picked hops from the ground to the slatted drying-floor of the oast-houses.

'Okay. I'll see to it. I'll drop the damaged plate in at the forge and collect it when we come back from Esther's.'

'Yes, Mister Tom.' Reuben nodded and was about to return to his machinery when he remembered something else. 'Oh, Mister Tom! You're wanted down at the packing-shed.'

Tom turned again. 'Urgently?'

Reuben raised a shoulder. 'Pace said to tell you he needs a word with you before midday.'

Tom sighed. 'All right, I'll find out what he wants.' He gave a lop-sided grin at Beth and muttered: 'And so the rich fabric of life winds itself more tightly round my neck . . . The old man is right: I shouldn't be skipping off with you.'

Beth threw him a quick glance. He was strong, but he was tired, and it was a tiredness that seemed more of the spirit than of the flesh.

'Nonsense,' she said briskly. 'The run to Esther's is all in the line of duty and you just told Reuben that you'd call at the forge, anyhow. That's killing two birds with one stone.' She frowned. 'You have your work cut out with the oasts; I'll sort out the packing-shed problem when we come back. It's probably only something to do with the piece-work rates for the plums.'

'You have the accounts to do, and a thousand and one things in the house, and the hens, and the eggs and — '

'I'll manage. If necessary, I'll rope in Lucy and we'll all burn the midnight oil,' laughed Beth.

Tom groaned. 'What I wouldn't give to

turn my back on this lot! Ironical, isn't it? Lucy would part with her eye-teeth for all this and it's me that's lumbered with the bloody place.'

'You're just tired and overworked, and T.J.'s being difficult, and — '

'Ain't life grand!' He linked his arm in hers and they threaded their way along beside the hopfield, where the hops hung among their dark leaves like tiny lime-green lamps. They found Jordan in the spot Reuben had indicated, swinging a billhook and cursing vociferously. He seemed quite happy to take himself back to the press.

'And now a-mowing we will go,' said Tom, giving Beth a wink.

Five minutes later he was studying the uncut acres of baked blond wheat with a fond, professional eye. 'Beautiful, isn't it? This is one experiment that seems to have paid off.' He took out a knife, stooped and sliced a smooth swathe. 'I prefer wheat, anyhow. Barley is a right b — ' He caught himself up. 'Barley is the devil to deal with. It's hard on the hands and, no matter how careful you are, the broken tips work into your clothes and scratch you to pieces.' A faint smile twisted his mouth. 'Which is probably the reason why the old man makes damned sure I always work the barley-fields.' He used the knife again, slicing the stems of wheat cleanly at their base. 'How much of this does Esther want?'

Beth shrugged. 'That should be enough, now. She prefers to use it freshly cut. I took her some a couple of days ago, but she's been showing the children how to make the dollies and they waste a lot.'

'Do you remember her teaching us? She started us off on a Bridget Cross, as I recall. And a right mess I made of it.'

'That was the year you cut your hand and bled over everything, and Archer — '

And Archer had stayed with the nearly demented Beth until her brother had been stitched together and handed safely back to her. Beth's lashes flickered. Gathering up the cut straw, she leaned against the open five-barred gate, her eyes on a butterfly which was sunning itself on one of the wooden support posts.

'Lucky butterfly, without a care under the sun.'

Tom stopped what he was doing and came to stand beside his sister. 'A Hedge Brown.' He watched the bright chestnut wings fan out in the sunshine. 'The Gatekeeper . . . You often see them like that, between gaps in the hedges, resting on the warm wood of the farm gates.' He bent and picked a poppy, threading it in Beth's hair, behind her ear, at the same time dropping half a handful of grain down the front of her blouse.

'Oh, you wretch,' gasped Beth, groping. She gave him a push, harder than he had been expecting for he was caught off balance and staggered into the hedge.

For a second he rocked, half-sitting, looking up at her, a surprised expression on his face, before beginning to struggle to his feet. Laughing, she snatched up an armful of straw and tossed it on top of him, then was off, still laughing, running down the side of the cornfield, among the poppies and corn-chamomile, and the rusting-seeded docks. But Tom was after her, running faster than she was and gaining at every step. He came behind her in a rush, knocking her to the ground and flinging himself on top of her on the soft flower-studded headland, where they rolled over and over in the long grass, like puppies, wriggling and kicking.

'Enough!' gasped Beth at last, spitting grass-seeds from her lips.

He spread himself over her, flattening her into the ground. She smelled of summer and sunshine and sun-warmed corn.

'Say you are sorry,' he commanded.

'No.'

He pressed harder. 'Go on. Say you are sorry.'

'Sorry,' she gasped. 'You brute.'

He rolled off and helped her to sit up and hugged her to him, laughing.

'You look like a moulting scarecrow,' he said, picking fragments of wheat-husk from her hair. For a few more moments he crouched beside her, removing the clinging debris from her clothes, then he relaxed at her feet and leaned back against her bent knees. Several minutes passed in sleepy silence as they contented themselves with looking at the view spread before them; the downs every shade of green and gold in the distance, mottled with light and shade, and the smell of hops like an anaesthetic under the sun. A distant sound of machinery and voices came hardly louder than the bees.

'This is the life,' murmured Tom. 'Listening to the rest of the world working.'

'One day,' said Beth drowsily, 'I'm going to spend a whole day like a butterfly, spread out in the sun.'

'And one day I'll join you.' His hand moved on her bare leg. 'Come on. Time we were going — or the old man'll be on the rampage again.'

Beth let him haul her to her feet.

3

Tom and Beth, having made a detour to drop the damaged bolt-plate from the elevator in at the forge, arrived at Elderwood about twenty minutes later. They pulled in and parked the Land-Rover beside a small orchard, where they could see Dewey, the village odd-job man, filling a sack with ripe plums. His bicycle was propped across the main gate. As the Channings rounded the obstacle and trod forward along the overgrown drive towards the house, the sharp crackle of breaking glass came to their ears, and the voices of children, squealing.

'What on earth's going on?' murmured Tom, hitching the bundle of corn he was carrying higher under his arm. 'It sounds like a riot.'

With some trepidation they headed for the side lawn and the noise. The crash of breaking glass came again, more loudly, and they turned a corner to find Esther

Deauville wielding a hammer and merrily smashing bottles in an old zinc bath. She was wearing a tweed skirt and sensible brogues, but the rest of her outfit, a waisted scarlet jacket with brass buttons, ancient motor-cycle goggles and a pair of large leather gauntlets, owed more to pantomime than to the Countrywoman's Guild.

Beside her a group of children giggled and worked and fought round a trestle-table erected on the grass, while a red-haired boy, aged about ten, was peppering all and sundry with ripe elderberries blown from a hollow elder-stem. Him Tom and Beth knew well. This was the notorious Georgie Mumford, scourge of all creatures great and small, and choir pest in particular, who lived with his sister and widowed mother in a cottage on the Channings' farm. Mrs Mumford did casual work in the orchards there and occasionally obliged at the Bell. She also rid herself of Georgie whenever, and wherever, possible.

Before Tom and Beth could make their presence known, half a dozen geese materialised behind them, running towards them from the direction of the orchard, honking menacingly, with their necks thrust forward, and pursued, in the far distance, by Dewey. Tom and Beth, old hands at this eyeball-to-eyeball confrontation, stood their ground and the geese came to a halt within a few inches of them, hissing, their outstretched necks weaving slowly from side to side.

Esther, who had looked up at the interruption, pushed the goggles to the top of her head and went past the two Channings at a gallop, flapping her hands and shooing the geese back the way they had come and screeching at Dewey to close the orchard gate after them. 'Damned old fool,' shouted Esther. 'Why did you leave it open?' She grabbed up a stick and whacked the ground to the rear of the last and largest goose, which seemed set fair to argue territorial rights with its mistress. Dewey moved sharply out of her way.

'Mad as a March hare,' he growled aside to Tom and Beth, who had followed along the drive in Esther's wake.

'Just like her ma.'

Silently they watched Esther deal with the rebel and fasten the gate firmly against the lashing beak.

'Cantankerous old cuss!' she hurled after the bird and returned to the three bystanders, still uttering imprecations, her face flushed and her hair escaping from its coils and hanging down her back. Although she was over seventy, her hair remained its original polished jet and betrayed her gipsy ancestry. 'If there's anything in the theory of reincarnation, that old buzzard was formerly Attila the Hun!' She pulled up a sleeve to show blue-black bruising the length of her forearm. 'That's what the wretch did to me yesterday. Nearly broke my arm. I can hardly use it, this morning.'

'Why don't you wring their bally necks?' said Tom.

'They're good watch-dogs,' replied Esther. 'Poor Pym's not up to much.' She jerked her head to where an aged, half-blind labrador was scratching itself in the sun. 'With the geese around, I know nobody can come near without my knowledge. And, when I'm alone at night, that's a comforting thought.' She tossed aside her stick. 'Not that this is another Kenlake House; I have nothing worth stealing. But a lone woman is always fair game for any thug.'

'Anyone in his right mind would think twice about tackling you, Esther,' smiled Tom.

'That's as may be, but I don't want too many shocks like yesterday,' rejoined Esther tartly. 'Nor do I wish to talk to another policeman for a long, long time.'

'Poor Esther. Did they ask you a lot of questions?'

'They gave me the fourth degree,' said Esther.

'Third degree, you mean.'

'I know what I mean and I know what they gave me,' snapped Esther. 'Tate, our local man, is harmless enough, but they brought in some smart detectives from Adford, with more paper qualifications than sense, who wanted to know why I'd touched the dead man and why I'd turned him over and whether I'd found anything on him, or near him. Perhaps they thought I'd rifled his pockets.' Her voice showed her disgust.

'I don't suppose they meant anything by it,' soothed Tom. 'That would be routine.'

'Ruddy foreigners,' put in Dewey, fastening his sack of plums on the back of his bicycle, 'tramping their big feet over everything and asking tom-fool questions — '

'I didn't know he was a dead man, did I?' said Esther, her tone aggrieved. 'Not until I'd touched him. And, even then, he was still warm so I turned him over to see if there was anything I could do for him. He was terribly injured; his face was a mass of raw flesh and his arm was ripped to shreds, but I thought — ' Her voice trailed off. Then she said: 'He was still warm, you see. But not breathing. He was lying, face down, in the water at the bottom of the ditch.'

'Do the police know how he came there?' asked Tom.

'If they do, they're keeping quiet,' replied Esther. 'I imagine his mates ran out on him, after he was hurt.'

'Dumped him, you mean?'

'It looks like it. Perhaps they were afraid he'd slow them up.'

Tom frowned. 'But according to the reports in the paper, from Kenlake House, the rest of the gang scarpered while the going was good and didn't wait around for — what was his name? Rolfe? — Their van was found abandoned near the quarry. Several people saw it en route and the police reckon the thieves had another vehicle already parked nearby and transferred themselves and their loot to that . . . And that's where the dead man must have been heading.'

'They left Rolfe to escape under his own steam?' queried Esther.

'It seems so,' said Tom. 'And in the condition he was evidently in it must have taken a superhuman effort to stagger as far as he did. Possibly he collapsed, unconscious, face down in that ditch and drowned, just before you found him.'

'The wicked shall be punished for their wickedness,' droned Dewey.

'Yes, very laudable,' said Esther. 'But I think I'd better go back to the children, or I shall need to be doing a bit of punishing on my own account: they're probably killing each other.'

'If you'd just move that bicycle, Dewey,' said Tom, 'I'll take Esther's poultry feed up and put it in her corn-bin,' He gave the battered machine a helping shove in the right direction and its rider wobbled slowly forward into the lane.

Turning, Dewey put one foot on the grass verge and called back: 'Perhaps now they'll go back where they came from. Ruddy foreigners and their ruddy money.' He spat into the hedge. 'And ruddy reporters. Ruddy strangers all over the place — ' he spat again over the wheel of the bicycle ' — buying up our goods and bunging up our streets. Why can't they all go home? We don't want them here.' Pushing off with his foot, he went wheeling idly round the first bend.

Esther cackled and spun on her heel. 'Talking of strangers, when are you going to bring the Newton lad to see me, young Beth?'

'As soon as I can prise him away from

his farm; but there's a lot to do. The old place was very neglected and Jeff's shorthanded at the moment.'

'Aren't we all?' said Tom.

Esther grimaced. 'Only a fool would be trying to make a go of that place. Still, I hear he's a nice boy.'

'Praise indeed,' said Beth, her tone dry. 'You'll like him. He's kind and he's easy-going. He reminds me of Tom.'

'I thought he might,' said Esther, watching Tom bump past them in the Land-Rover.

Beth gave the old woman a hard stare, suspecting more than the surface sarcasm. Tall and upright still, in her younger days Esther must have been a striking woman, with the sloe-black hair and the strongly-carved features of her gipsy forebears. But it was when she turned full face that the shock came. Her eyes, under brows straight and black as a raven's wing, were not the obsidian one somehow expected, nor were they the Deauville blue, but a startling, golden marigold that gleamed on the world with ill-concealed mockery. Her memory was still perfect, her judgements caustic and without mercy, and she had a tongue like a meat-chopper.

Her father, Richard Deauville, had been the biggest land-owner in the district; her mother, Esther Colley, a gipsy girl, beautiful, wilful and a member of the same family from which Reuben and Jordan Colley had later sprung. It had been a love-match, short and passionate and defiant, and the village had been scandalised — not by the fact that Richard Deauville had succumbed to flashing eyes and a ripely fair body, but that he had married her. Their happiness, if happiness there was, had been brief. Within two years the first Esther was showing signs of imbalance, within three she was totally deranged. She died before the younger Esther was ten.

Beth stooped and gathered up the sheaf of corn which Tom had dumped on the lawn when they had retraced their steps to the orchard gate. Following Esther, she carried her burden across to a bench by the east wing of the house. To one side, a flight of broken steps led down to what had been the original cellar. Fire-blackened masonry graced the upper walls; the cellar door was new, strong and bolted. Beside it, piled in a tiny pyre, were some branches from an elder tree, recently cut, the toothed leaves just beginning to wilt.

Once Elderwood had been one of the most beautiful houses in the area. The marble-pillared portico with its fine sweep of shallow, semi-circular steps, the carved stone urns and balustrades, the upthrust of perfectly-proportioned windows, pointed a little to the grandeur that had gone. Fire had destroyed the greater part of the house, neglect had done the rest and through those lovely naked windows there could be seen only weeds: nettles and brambles and young elder-trees, all fighting for footholds among the hunks of tumbled stone. Only the east wing of the house remained roofed and comparatively undamaged and it was there that Esther lived now, alone.

Even before her father died, and long before the fire had taken its toll, the estate had been in difficulties and most of the farmland had been sold to pay off debts; while the new motorway had sliced through the little acreage remaining so that the house was left high and dry and almost landless. Esther had retained her orchard and a couple of small fields on the northern side, rented out to a neighbouring farmer, and a large unspoiled tract of woodland which connected with the Reads' farm to the west. There was also the rambling garden, where flowers and fruit-bushes ran such glorious riot that the scuffling feet of scores of children made as much impact as monkeys in an Amazonian jungle.

Esther growled: 'Beth, give me a hand with this, would you — over to the bench.' She indicated the zinc bath with its pieces of broken bottle.

'What's that for?' asked Beth.

'I'm making glass plaques for the church bazaar.' She handed Beth a circular object the size of a dinner-plate and so heavy that Beth almost dropped it. There appeared to be a multi-hued design worked on it, mosaic-fashion, in coloured glass. It was not until Beth held it up and the light shone through the clear backing that the full effect could be seen. Suddenly the drab, lumpy disc was transformed by colour, in the way a stained-glass window inside a church leaps to life in the sun, with glowing reds and golds and greens spilling a butterfly brightness across her sleeve. The picture she held was of poppies and corn; the red, like blood, pouring over her hand.

'It's lovely,' said Beth. She picked up another plaque and held it into the sun and the picture sprang forward, vibrantly. An emerald-green and sapphire-blue peacock with a spread tail, its head raised arrogantly, tipped with bronze. Another, in shades of gold, represented the church, with its conspicuous spire. 'They're very unusual, Esther.'

'I don't suppose you've any red bottles you don't want, have you?' asked Esther. She groped around among the pieces of glass in the bath. 'I can find plenty of green and brown and amber, but red and blue are scarce.'

'I'll have a look when I get home. We might have something.'

'And I need some more hops,' said Esther, 'for hop-pillows. But picked by hand, not by that smelly machine.'

'I'll see what I can do,' promised Beth. 'I suppose they are for the church bazaar, too?'

Esther nodded, still searching among her pieces of broken glass.

Beth left her to her task and wandered across the grass to examine the corn dollies Esther and the children had been making. A group of older girls sat demurely weaving the straw into complicated traditional designs, pausing now and again to choose and attach a ribbon from the many-coloured heap upon the table. Among others, Beth recognised the long, twisted-handle shape of the Nek, the square Bridget Cross, and the more difficult to produce, but very attractive, drop dolly, with its cousin, common to that area and which she had found nowhere else, the Kentish Lantern. The younger children had long ago given up their labours with equal relief and rapidity and were pelting each other with heads of corn.

'Stop that,' said Esther sharply to them, arriving at Beth's elbow. 'If you want to play, move away from the table.' Glancing down, she spotted the corn dolly in Beth's hand. 'Go on,' she said. 'Try your skill. See if you remember how.'

'I could hardly forget,' laughed Beth. 'I still make them every year, for Harvest Festival. Is that what this lot is for?'

'No,' replied Esther. 'Although they are to decorate the church — along with the glass plaques and any other craft-work the rector can drum up. He wants them for the festival concert first and then they will be returned to sell on the stalls at the bazaar. To impress Ingham's sophisticated singer with our rustic talents.' She gave one of her harsh cackles of laughter. 'Doubtless it will merely confirm her opinion that we're a bunch of hayseeds. Did you know that the grand lady's agreed to open our bazaar? She must enjoy punishment.'

'The proceeds are for the church, so she could hardly refuse.'

'She's asked for a small sum to be set aside to provide an outing for the dear little children.' Esther smiled around her sourly and caught sight of the red-haired boy standing on his head. 'Georgie Mumford, you'll mash your brains,' she said. 'And, seeing that you are one of those who will benefit from the rake-off, isn't it about time you did some work, if you intend staying here?'

He flipped the right way up, face redder than his hair and growled: 'I ain't making no rotten straw dollies. That's cissie.'

'That's just where you're wrong, young man,' said Esther, hauling him to his feet and stuffing a cluster of cornstalks in his unwilling hands. 'In times past it used to be the men who made these dollies — and sometimes in a far more violent manner than you'd ever dream of. Isn't that right, Tom?' She appealed to Beth's brother who had finished stowing the grain and had walked across to stand beside them.

'Yes,' said Tom. 'Corn dollies were part of the ancient fertility rites.'

'What's them?' asked Georgie, suspiciously.

'Well — sort of rituals for the renewal of life and the re-growth of the corn,' said Tom, sliding out of that one dextrously. 'The ribbons represent various things; red for the poppies and gold for the corn goddess, Ceres, for example. Even the name doesn't necessarily mean a dolly, as you're thinking of it. It could be a corruption of the word 'idol'. Very pagan. Which should suit you down to the ground, my lad.'

'I bet you never made any of them,' said Georgie, a little less rebelliously.

'That's where you're again wrong. Esther taught me how to make corn dollies when I was no bigger than you. Look, I'll show you — if I can remember.'

Esther watched his big hands fumble the straw. 'Ye gods!' she said at last, when he had finished and balanced his lop-sided effort on the table, her faith in Tom's ability as guide and mentor considerably shaken. 'As a weaver of straw you'd make a very fine demolition worker. But then you always were ham-fisted. Archer could turn out better stuff, left-handed.'

66

'Archer Read was always good with his hands,' said Tom smoothly.

Esther glanced at him sharply. 'I hear he's doing well at the mill.'

'So they say,' said Tom.

'The whole project seems a bit pointless to me,' sniffed Esther. 'Like trying to turn back the clock.'

'I think we should all aim to do that,' put in Beth. 'Preserve a little of what once was, I mean, before it decays and goes for ever. And people enjoy seeing the windmill grinding corn, the place is quite a tourist attraction.'

'Some people will gawp at anything,' retorted Esther. 'Besides, if Archer's doing anything with that mill, it's far more likely to be for his own ends than for the good of future generations, or conservation, or love of nature.' She shot a hard glance at Tom. 'I hear he's taken up with Melinda, now. I thought she was your girl?'

'What Melinda does is her affair,' said Tom. He didn't look too put out.

Esther scowled. 'You should try a little backbone occasionally.'

'Do you think she's worth it?' replied Tom, giving her a grin.

'Well, you won't hold on to a girl while you trail around with your sister . . . Georgie Mumford!' Her voice rose to a shriek. 'Come away from that cellar door.'

Georgie did as he was bid, reluctantly. He didn't quite know what he wanted to do, but it wasn't anything Esther wanted. He kicked a plant-pot in passing.

'Hello, Georgie,' smiled Beth. 'Why aren't you with Mr Waterhouse and the choirboys this morning?'

'I had to bring Sharon up here,' he said sullenly, indicating a small plump girl with a round face, who was sitting winding ribbons on the lawn.

'You've done that,' said Esther tartly. 'You can go home.'

'Sharon wants me to stay.' He scuffed the toe of his shoe into the grass, digging dirt.

'No, I don't!' The small freckled face looked up indignantly. 'Mummy is coming for me later.'

'The rector is giving you boys a guided

tour of the church,' said Beth, her voice coaxing. 'Telling you about the brasses and the font and the stained-glass windows. It's all very interesting.'

'No, it ain't.' Georgie dug a larger hole with his toe.

'They're climbing inside the church spire,' volunteered Sharon, looking up again. 'There's a little platform, way up near the top where you can see — ' she puffed importantly ' — three countries.'

'Counties, dim-wit,' snapped the amiable George.

'Well, you don't want to miss all that excitement, do you?' said Tom. 'We're going into the village, you can ride with us.'

'Can I?' He looked at Tom. Tom was his idol. Tom, quite effortlessly, held the allegiance of most of the village young.

'Certainly. We have to collect a piece of machinery from the forge.'

'Good.' Georgie smiled for the first time that day.

'Then find your jacket,' said Esther quickly, before he could change his mind. She watched him run across the lawn.

69

'For that act of charity, Tom, thank you. That boy is the original fly in everybody's ointment ... A tsetse fly,' she added bitterly.

'Oh, I don't know,' replied Tom. 'He's all right if handled properly.'

'Then he can go and be handled elsewhere.' She glanced at the man at her side. 'Tom, might I ask you to do another Samaritan deed for me, before you go?' He turned to her enquiringly. 'You know the big elder-tree? The one by the house? Would you hack out the roots for me? I've sawn the stock down as far as I can, but I can't manage the rest.' She led Tom across to the flight of broken steps and the pile of cut branches with their dying leaves and dropping berries.

He surveyed the scene for a moment, in silence. Then said: 'That tree's been here as long as I can remember, Esther.'

'I'm asking you to dig it out, not weep over it,' she said irritably. 'It has a penchant for my drains.'

'Okay. If that's what you want. But it'll have to wait until this evening. It looks like a pretty substantial job to me and I shan't be able to manoeuvre a mechanical digger down there.'

'Can you do it?'

He nodded. 'Tonight. When things slacken off a bit at the farm. I can't stay any longer now, or I'll be for the high jump.'

Esther snorted. 'T.J. doesn't know when he's well off.'

'I think he does,' said Tom ruefully. 'It's when he's got me leaping like a fire-cracker.' He stared for a moment longer at the remains of the tree, then ran his eyes over the new cellar-door. 'That's a nice piece of timber, Esther, solid as a ship. What do you keep down there? The crown jewels?'

'That, Tom Channing, is none of your business,' rapped Esther. And she strode swiftly across the lawn to make sure Georgie had been secured in the Land-Rover.

4

'That's old Petticoats, aint it?' husked Georgie's nasal voice, as his head thrust between Tom and Beth. He was kneeling in the back of the Land-Rover, peering forward, his elbows alternately either resting along the top of their seats or digging into their spines.

'If you mean Miss Pettifer, full marks for observation,' retorted Tom dryly. 'And get your bally elbow out of my ear.' He was already drawing the vehicle to a halt beside the small trudging figure. 'Hello, Vi. Can we give you a lift? We're going as far as the village.'

Violet Pettifer skipped across to his window. 'That's very kind of you, Tom. I won't say no. I've been on the trot since eight o'clock this morning.'

'Picking blackberries?' queried Tom, eyeing the stained plastic bag in her hand. 'There are plenty of those by our lower wood, if you want to try there, nearer home. There'll be a bumper crop this year, given a couple more weeks' ripening weather.' He swung down to the road to help her up into the Land-Rover beside Beth.

'All right, Tom,' said Violet, fending him off. 'I'll climb in the back with Georgie, if you'll just wait until I collect my other bags.'

Georgie scowled.

'And what might you be doing here, young Georgie?' she asked brightly, leaning forward. Georgie scowled harder and, not waiting for his answer, Violet tripped back across the verge and further along the hedgerow and began rummaging under the bushes.

'Nosy cow,' muttered Georgie.

'Hush, Georgie. She'll hear you,' admonished Beth.

'Good,' said Georgie, unrepentant. 'Nosy old cow.'

A neat, sturdy woman in her mid-fifties and an inveterate gossip, Violet Pettifer knew all there was to be known in Otley Ash. She possessed her own system of supply and demand in information and the village grapevine was acknowledged to be firmly rooted in her cottage. Yet, for all her faults, there was no malice in her and she brought the same boundless energy to her worthy causes that she gave to her clacking tongue.

'I didn't come out here intending to pick blackberries,' she called back, over her shoulder. 'I wanted some mushrooms, but I didn't have much luck.' She retrieved a bag and held it towards Tom. Two small mushrooms nestled at the bottom. 'Pathetic, isn't it? And to think that we used to gather hundreds of them.'

'The weather's not been good for mushrooming,' ventured Tom. 'Too dry.'

'The fault lies with that beastly motorway,' said Violet hotly 'It's carved through all the mushroom meadows and ruined them. Ingham Read always allowed me to take as many as I wanted from Ten Acre, but that's gone now, under concrete. I was down by the Titanic this morning and there wasn't a solitary mushroom to be seen.'

Tom accepted this statement, nodding.

The Titanic was the local name for the motorway bridge recently built on Esther's lower meadows where they joined Ingham's property, near the river Addot, and reputed once more to be sinking. Its construction had been complicated by local springs and underground reservoirs and eventually the main river itself had had to be rerouted, only to find that, although the bridge might now stand securely, many other things would not. The first rains had swollen the new Addot to a torrent, flooding six fields, five cottages, two roads and a dene-hole, and the area outcry had been such that someone in authority had quickly thrown up the bright idea of yet another diversion to the main river, and a brand-new sluice. And the necessity for webbed feet had receded.

Tom said: 'If you want mushrooms, you're welcome to try Larks' Meadow, behind our hopfields. They used to grow there in great quantities at one time.'

'May I?' Violet looked pleased. 'Thank you. They're my favourite dish and I really am an awful pig over them.'

'Oink, oink,' said Georgie, indistinctly to their rear.

Tom raised a shoulder and pulled a wry face at the woman beside him. 'Are you sure you fancy riding in the back with him?'

'Georgie Mumford's rudeness doesn't worry me,' said Violet. 'He takes after his father and we all know what he was like.' She thrust another bag into Tom's hands. 'Watercress,' she explained, as she bent to grovel once more beneath the hedge. A moment later she hauled yet another large bag from its hiding-place and promptly showered the contents at Tom's feet as the plastic ripped on a spike of blackthorn.

'Oh! Oh! Oh!' she wailed, staring down at the scattered blackberries.

'We'll soon pick them up,' said Tom, scooping his hands full of the berries and looking around for somewhere to put them.

'Here,' said Beth, running across to them with an empty cardboard box. 'Fill that.' She knelt and, neatly and quickly, began to help her brother and Violet rescue the fallen fruit. The mishap had done it little good. Many of the berries, especially those fielded by Tom, were squashed and oozing dark juice.

'Never mind,' said Tom philosophically, 'they'll still make a nice pie.'

'Pie . . . ? Oh, yes,' said Violet. Her hands stopped fluttering across the berries and she glanced up at him, then said abruptly: 'Have you read your newspaper this morning, Tom?'

He stared back at her, surprised. 'Yes, fleetingly — Why?'

'I wondered if you'd spotted the article on the Kenlake House robbery? The police have found the thieves' van. In the old quarry.'

'Oh, that,' said Tom. 'Yes, I read that. Not surprising they found the vehicle, really; they'd received a good description of it from Kenlake House.'

'I think I saw it too, that afternoon, after the robbery.'

Tom stared at her again. 'You did?'

'Yes, I believe so.'

'Well, I suppose that's not so strange, either. Several people reported seeing the van then and it would have had to come this way to the quarry. The police assume the men had another getaway vehicle planted nearby and transferred to that.'

'But wouldn't they have taken their loot with them?' Violet sounded puzzled.

Tom laughed. 'Yes, of course. They wouldn't leave the stuff behind after all the effort they went through to lift it.'

'In their pockets?' Violet's tone was still unsure.

'I hardly think so,' said Tom, with another laugh. 'One of the items was reported to be a knee-high silver statu-ette.' He looked down at her. 'What's worrying you?'

'I'm not sure. But I'm almost certain that it must have been the thieves' van I saw. Blue, and with the registration PYE something or other, the paper says, and I remember that, because I had a pie ready to put in the oven when I got back, and — '

'Whereabouts did you see this van? On the road?'

'No. That was the odd thing. It was drawn up under the hedge, just inside a farm gate along Bower Lane, near the new motorway banking there. It couldn't be seen from the lane itself, but I'd come across the field path . . . ' She frowned. 'Anyhow, three men jumped out and scrambled up the banking and disappeared and I thought I heard an engine start, but I guessed I must have imagined it because that part of the road isn't in use yet. Anyway, I waited a while.'

'Near the van?'

'No. I carried on walking, but I kept the top of the motorway banking in sight. I was sure the men would be coming back and I wondered what it was they could be doing on the unfinished road.' She gave a little embarrassed giggle. 'I was pretty sure it was all very innocent. You know!' She glanced at Tom from under her lashes, blushing. 'They wanted to — you know.'

'On the new motorway?' said Tom with incredulity.

'I thought it was a bit strange, there being plenty of hedges and trees and bushes around, but men are peculiar creatures,' said Violet, with the air of one who found the ways of the opposite sex totally incomprehensible.

'Not that peculiar,' said Tom.

'Well, they didn't' said Violet.

Tom and Beth stared at her, wide-eyed.

'They didn't come back to the van, I mean,' said Violet crossly. 'I waited ages, but they never returned.'

'You must have missed them,' said Tom.

Violet shook her head. 'I'm positive I didn't.'

'Then,' said Beth slowly, 'you believe you saw the Kenlake House thieves in the process of transferring to their new vehicle?'

Violet wriggled. 'That crossed my mind later, only — '

'Why didn't you tell the police?' cut in Tom.

'I thought I must have been mistaken. You see, everyone was saying that they'd stolen such a lot of stuff, over two million pounds' worth of antiques and jewellery and such.' She looked at Tom accusingly. 'You yourself just told me that they couldn't have carried it off in their pockets.'

'So?'

'Then they didn't take it with them,' said Violet defiantly. 'If those three men I saw really were the thieves, they carried nothing with them, nothing at all.'

'They must have done. Bags, boxes, sacks — something.'

'I tell you they didn't.' Two spots of crimson showed on Violet's cheeks. 'I'm neither blind nor stupid, and those men carried nothing at all. Each one used both his hands to help him climb the steep banking — you know what it's like there. A stiff haul. If they had the proceeds of the robbery with them, then they left it in the van.' She looked from one to the other. 'And it must have been the same van the police were looking for, mustn't it? PYE? Surely, it would be too much of a coincidence for there to be another, there, at that time?'

'I would say so,' said Tom. 'But it was found in the quarry. The men must have returned to it, later. Perhaps when darkness came.'

Violet shook her head. 'I nipped back there myself, when they seemed to be such a long time returning. Out of curiosity.' Her voice was sheepish. 'And the van had gone.'

Tom said firmly: 'There you are then. They must have left a driver in it — if they really were connected with the Kenlake House robbery — to hide the goods and dispose of the van.'

'No.' Violet looked a little shamefaced. 'I'd already checked the first time, as I walked past. There was no one there. Someone else must have come along and driven it off.'

'Someone who dropped from the sky?' queried Tom, a touch of irritation in his voice.

'Tom! Don't be unkind,' murmured Beth.

'Did you see anyone else, Vi?' demanded Tom. 'Or another vehicle?'

'No, but someone could have parked further along the lane, or walked that way. Or come across the fields . . .'

'Yes,' said Tom. 'Or flown in on the wings of a dove.'

'And I'll tell you something else,' retorted Violet with spirit. 'The van didn't drive off in the direction of the quarry, either, or it would have passed me.'

Tom stared at her, startled, but before he could speak Georgie's indignant voice shrilled from the back of the Land-Rover.

'Come on, you lot. Hurry up.' He banged the side of the truck.

Beth picked up the box of blackberries and walked across to him. 'Put those by your feet,' she said. 'And don't tread on them.'

Georgie sniffed. 'It looks as if someone's already trodden on them.'

'Yes, well . . . '

'I suppose I shall have to tell the police?' said Violet reluctantly, at her elbow.

'I don't see how you can avoid it,' said Beth. 'Your information might be of some help to them.'

'I can't stand those detectives from Adford,' Violet muttered. 'They make me nervous. I wouldn't mind if it were just Jim Tate I had to deal with.'

'Call in and see him, then,' said Beth.

'I tried this morning,' countered Violet. 'But he wasn't there.'

'No, he's over at Connington, today,' put in Tom. 'Something to do with sheep-rustling on the farms around there, I believe.'

'That's that, then,' sighed Violet. 'He'd probably only hand me over to his superiors, anyway. I might as well save him the bother.'

Tom looked at her troubled face. 'I'm bound to see Tate tonight, in the Bell,' he said gently. 'I'll have a word with him myself, if you like, and ask him to drop by your place tomorrow.'

'Would you?' Violet perked up. 'Thank you, Tom, I'd appreciate that.'

Georgie hung over the tailgate. 'Police? What d'you want the police for?'

'Never you mind,' said Violet severely. 'And stop scratching your head, it's disgusting. You were doing it in church last Sunday and everyone was staring. I'm sure they all thought your hair was full of livestock: I heard Miss Deauville remark that we needed a nature warden.' She moved to climb into the rear of the

Land-Rover, but Tom checked her, laughing.

'Take the passenger seat, Vi, I'll ride with our fidgety friend. Beth can drive.' He grinned at his sister. 'Besides, seeing that I've been gone a lot longer than I intended, I think I'd better leave you lovely ladies at the farm-turning and dash off and do some work, or T.J. will be creating an international incident. You won't mind collecting the boltplate for me, Beth, will you? It should be ready.'

Beth nodded and waved him off at the end of the track that led to Channings.

'He's a good lad, your brother,' said Violet. 'He'll do anything for anyone. Not like some I could mention.' She peered ahead. 'I'm supposed to be making jam this afternoon. Dewey was to bring me some plums from Esther Deauville's. Which reminds me, young Georgie — ' she turned ' — you were to call in yesterday with half a dozen jam-jars from your mother. What happened?'

'I forgot,' growled Georgie.

'Well, remember this afternoon.'

'We saw Dewey with the fruit,' said

Beth. 'He's probably left it on your step by now.'

'Yes,' said Violet grimly. 'And himself with it, if I know Dewey. He's been hired to cut my hedge today.'

Which was not exactly what Dewey was doing when they pulled up at Violet Pettifer's neat white weather-boarded cottage a few minutes later. His bicycle was propped against a shed, the sack of plums stood on the lawn and Dewey was lolling in a large wheelbarrow, smoking. As Violet walked through the gate, he sprang to his feet, grabbed a pair of shears and began to snip industriously at the hedge.

Beth smiled to herself as she acknowledged Violet's wave of thanks and pulled away.

The Pettifer cottage was on the outskirts of the village, well back from the road, and it was several more minutes before the Land-Rover reached the village proper and drew in beside the duck-pond with its vivid cover of green weed. The church lay a short distance beyond the water, on a grassy rise, and Beth was just in time to see the rector and a bevy of small boys vanish within the west porch.

'Run, Georgie,' she said. 'You can't have missed much.'

He trailed away from her across the grass, reluctantly it seemed, dragging his jacket behind him. Beth did not wait to see him clasped to Mr Waterhouse's welcoming bosom, but set off again towards the forge, on the far side of the village. Her errand there quickly completed, she collected a few things from the one and only shop boasted by Otley Ash, and then returned along the main street, past the church, where an all-too-familiar red-haired figure was swinging on the lychgate. Beth frowned and brought the Land-Rover to a curving halt beside the pond once more.

5

By the time she had climbed out and made her way to the church gate, Georgie had disappeared. Eventually Beth found him perched on one of the bolster-shaped tombstones in the older part of the churchyard. He looked a strangely desolate figure sitting there, picking lichen from the grey stone. Even his vivid hair seemed subdued, its vibrant colour muted by the shadows of the crowding yews.

'There are less unpleasant places to sit, Georgie,' remarked Beth, seating herself beside him.

He raised one shoulder, not looking at her, and continued picking at his stone.

'Don't you want to go into the church with Mr Waterhouse?'

'Nope.'

'Your friends are in there,' persisted Beth.

'So?' He turned his head and glared at her. 'They'll come out again, won't they?'

Beth handed him a packet of sweets. 'Here; have a fruit gum. And for goodness' sake let's sit in the sun.'

Georgie accepted the offer ungraciously, then followed her across into the sunshine, where they squatted side by side on warm marble.

'Silly twits,' he said, conversationally, 'scrambling up inside church steeples.'

Beth looked up to where the slender, ornamented spire of Saint Mary's needled the noonday sky, 'And don't you want to go up there?'

'Nope.'

Communication languished while he finished the remainder of the fruit gums.

'I expect they're at the top now,' muttered Georgie, at last, hurling a stone. 'Stupid, I call it. What d'they want to climb old steeples for?' He hurled another stone.

'You'll break a church window if you're not careful,' said Beth mildly.

'Good. Serve him right. Serve the old bat right.' Georgie scowled upwards, but ceased his stone-throwing. 'I might just as well be back at home.'

'You might at that,' agreed Beth peaceably. 'I'll give you a lift, if you like.'

'My mates are all up there.'

'Hi! Geor . . . gie!' Voices floated faint and far away on the sunny air.

Georgie stared resolutely at his feet.

'I think your friends are trying to attract your attention,' said Beth, waving up at the cluster of heads near the top of the spire. She could just make out the spider railing that circled the narrow platform. 'There's the rector: you can see his black cassock.'

Georgie snorted. 'I hope he falls off.' He studied, very hard, a bee on a tuft of self-heal by his feet.

Beth followed his gaze. 'That's a cuckoo-bee,' she said.

'Uh?' Georgie flung her a startled glance. 'What? That fat old bumble-bee?'

'It's not a bumble-bee; the colouring is different. See that foxy flash at the front, the same shade as your hair? It's a cuckoo-bee. It doesn't build a nest and care for its young itself. It behaves like the cuckoo.'

'You mean it lays its eggs in some other bee's nest?'

'That's right. It chooses a bumble-bee nest and kills their queen and takes over. The cuckoo-bee's eggs are then cared for by the bumble-bee workers.'

For a few moments Georgie studied the insect with interest. But his grievance was too great to be suppressed for long.

'He's potty.'

'That's the way nature made him, I guess,' said Beth.

Georgie stared at her in disgust. 'Not that old cuckoo-bee thing; I mean Mr Waterhouse. Mr Waterhouse is potty.'

'The rector is very good to you. He works hard to make your holidays interesting.'

Georgie sighed. 'He's always taking us up things or down things,' he said. 'Last week it was up Reads' windmill. Right up and out to stand on that little platform at the back.'

'By the fantail? There's a lovely view from there.' Beth saw his face. 'But you didn't go?'

'Nope. Got better things to do with my

time.' He kicked a gravestone viciously. 'And before that it was down some silly old dene-hole — '

'He took you down Little Tott?'

'No. He said that was damaged in the flood. Big Tott, right over by Connington. And nothing to see when we got there, only dirty old chalk. Then the week before it was up some old look-out tower, or other.' He snarled: 'I didn't go there, either. And now they're all up there.' He jerked his head towards the spire.

'Never mind. I think they're coming down now, anyway,' said Beth, as the last of the heads disappeared from view. But she had suddenly seen the light. She glanced down at the bright brush at her side. 'Are you afraid of heights?'

'Nope,' said Georgie defiantly, reddening.

'Tom dislikes heights,' said Beth. 'Climbing towers isn't his idea of fun, either.'

'Tom?' Georgie's head swung round. 'Don't Tom like going up things? Up high, I mean?'

'No,' said Beth. 'He hates it. He gets

giddy if he stands on a step-ladder. But lots of people suffer with vertigo, it's nothing to be ashamed of.'

'Oh.' Georgie digested for a moment, then confided in a rush. 'I don't like being up high. It makes me feel bad, real bad. Only, you won't let that lot know, will you? They might laugh.'

'That's your secret, then,' said Beth. 'Listen, I think I can hear your friends coming.' There was a clatter of feet and a rush of voices and the group of boys erupted from a door at the side of the church. The Reverend Waterhouse brought up the rear.

'Good afternoon, Bethany,' he greeted her. The only person in the entire village ever to call her and her sister, Lucille, by their given baptismal names. 'How's T.J. today?'

'Pretty miserable,' said Beth. 'His foot's painful again and the hop-picking machine has broken down.'

'I'm sorry to hear it. Will he be coming to our church festival-concert on Friday?'

'I doubt it,' said Beth. 'He's not keen on music.'

'Oh, well — ' The rector's head swivelled as a golden goddess wafted by with swinging hair and lovely legs. The gorgeous Melinda, bearing flowers. Georgie eyed the tight little behind with approval and gave vent to a piercing whistle.

Mr Waterhouse bent his eyes on the boy. 'Hello, Georgie. Too late again, I see, for our little tour. But just in time for the nice picnic lunch Mrs Waterhouse will have ready for us. Come along.'

Georgie mumbled something incomprehensible and raced ahead to fight with a friend in the rectory garden.

'A strange boy,' remarked the rector, taking his leave of Beth. He put up a hand to his wife who was galloping across the grass towards them. 'Just coming, my dear.'

'It's Beth I want,' said Mrs Waterhouse, going past him at a tidy trot. She grabbed Beth's arm as she fought for breath. 'Glad I caught you,' she gasped. 'Your mother said you were somewhere in the village . . . ' Beth waited. 'I phoned to ask her for help with the trestle-tables. We

94

need them collected and delivered to the rectory, ready for the bazaar next week.'

'Yes?' said Beth guardedly, knowing that her services must already have been volunteered.

'Your mother says you have the Land-Rover with you and that you wouldn't mind collecting the tables and bringing them here now. Someone will help you load the iron trestles at the other end.' The rector's wife gave the girl a dazzling smile. 'I do hope we're not putting you to too much trouble.'

'No,' said Beth. 'That's all right.' One didn't argue with a bulldozer. 'Where am I to collect them from?'

'From Reads' mill. They were stored there after the summer fête at the Manor.'

Beth looked at her, aghast. 'From Reads' mill?' she echoed faintly.

'Yes. They're expecting someone to call. No problem. Your mother said to bring her back a sack of their stone-ground flour.' Mrs Waterhouse turned briskly. 'I must go. I'm feeding the five thousand.' And she galloped back across the grass leaving Beth staring after her in horror. After all that had happened, how on earth could she present herself at Reads' mill? But there was no way out.

Gritting her teeth, Beth drove through the village, past the forge, out into the green and gold countryside once more, and swung upwards along the lane towards Otley Manor. The hedges on either side of her were a riot of large white convolvulus flowers and pigeons were calling from the woods. Here and there a sheet of wild clematis showed ashy-green, its pods not yet ripened into the old man's beard which would trail like smoke through autumn and beyond.

Otley Manor, set overlooking its lovely gardens, a ha-ha, parkland and the Weald of Kent, showed little of the ravages of time. Clever and restless, with the gift of turning everything he touched to his advantage, Ingham Read could afford its upkeep, and the well-groomed drive and manicured lawns, and the banks of late summer flowers flaming in the herbaceous borders, all spoke of money freely spent.

Ingham Read himself was standing by

the sundial in the centre of the gravelled sweep that fronted the house. Beth parked the Land-Rover and walked across to him.

'Beth, my dear. How wonderful to see you!' He held out both hands to her in an extravagant gesture. Everything about Ingham was theatrical and larger than life, thought Beth. But there was no denying that he was still a very handsome man. Graceful and immaculate, he favoured a small pointed beard, greying now, like his dark hair, which gave him a swashbuckling Edmond Dantes look that suited his strong bone-structure. His eyes were a greenish grey; his hands, beautiful. Women, on the whole, found him delightful; but, after the death of his third wife more than a decade ago, he no longer put himself out to marry them.

'Good-day, Ingham,' said Beth.

'Beth. It's been far too long — ' He pulled her towards him and for an instant Beth thought he was going to kiss her and twisted her face away. She caught the whiff of something sharp and expensive. Then he let her go. He stood looking at her appraisingly. 'You grow lovelier every time I see you — the epitome of summer standing there. You have a certain glowing quality that is quite irresistible.'

Beth laughed outright at this blatant flattery. 'Then you'll be devastated by Lucy: she is the beauty of the family.'

'Ah, yes. Lovely Lucy, who has promised to delight us with her company . . . My dear, couldn't I persuade you to come to our little get-together on Thursday, to meet our celebrated diva?'

Beth stammered her excuses and explained her present errand.

Ingham nodded. 'The trestle-tables are in an outbuilding by the mill. Bring the Land-Rover round and Archer will load them for you.'

The Reads' smock mill was expertly preserved and in working order, although at the moment the shuttered sweeps stood idle against the blue sky. A fine layer of flour covered everything, like dust, and there was a rich nutty smell pervading the air. To the left of the mill was an old stable, with a cushion of catmint by its split-hinged door. Two cats wallowed there. To the right was a long low storage building with double doors folded back against the wall. An upturned barrel with a thermos flask on it stood just outside.

'Archer!' Ingham called, but made no attempt to enter the mill. He brushed a speck of flour from his sleeve.

Archer Read came through the doorway, blinking as he stepped into the bright sunshine. He held a half eaten sandwich in one hand and shot a scowling look of enquiry at his father. Then his eyes, becoming used to the brightness, slid past Ingham and fell on Beth. If he changed colour it would have been impossible to tell, his face was filmed pale with flour. But the eyes in their rims of dust, gleamed greenly, like a cat's. He took a step towards her.

'What the devil are you doing here? Slumming?' There was no mistaking the dislike in the accompanying cold stare. Apart from the eyes, which were a changeable greenish grey like Ingham's, he bore slight resemblance to his father. A certain grace when he moved, perhaps; a similar cut to the jaw, but with none of Ingham's easy charm. He was altogether stronger, harder, his mouth already marred with obstinacy.

Beth opened her lips to explain her presence but Ingham forestalled her.

'Beth's arrived to collect the trestle-tables for the bazaar,' he said. 'And some flour for her mother.'

'Has she really? The tables are over there.' Archer nodded towards the stable.

'I'm sorry to trouble you,' said Beth.

'I'm sure you are.'

'His manners don't expand with age, I'm afraid,' said Ingham to Beth, 'only his bad temper.' He swung round on his son. 'I presume you don't intend to let Beth carry the things herself?'

Again a gleam from the catlike eyes. 'And I presume you don't intend to soil your hands?'

'Unfortunately, I have to dash,' said Ingham lightly. 'Beth will forgive me if I rush away, I know, but business calls.'

The muscles in Archer's jaw tightened. 'Well, just before you go,' he said, 'I'd like a word with you. The flour count doesn't

tally. What are these orders doing here?'
He walked across to the storage bay and
pointed.

'That's a bulk order for Cavies,' said
Ingham. 'It's stamped on the sacks in
bold enough print if you'd bother to open
your eyes.'

'And who the hell are Cavies?'

'They're new customers. Important
ones, with valuable contacts.'

'It would have helped if you'd told me
sooner,' snapped Archer. 'How am I
supposed to run this place?'

'Oh, you'll find a way . . . You always
do.' Ingham turned away, but Archer
came after him, furiously.

'Will you leave things alone! Butt out! I
haven't the manpower or the time to fulfil
the orders I have already.'

'Keep your shirt on, boy, I was only
trying to help. Cavies supply Mossops'
chain of food stores.'

'I don't give a damn if they supply
Buckingham Palace. I am in charge here.'

'They will be good customers. Bring
big orders.'

Archer exploded. 'How many more

101

times do I have to tell you that I don't want any more big orders? I'm working flat out now. I've as much as the mill can cope with. It's not a mechanical marvel, you know. If you'd let me have a couple of men — '

'Can't be spared,' said Ingham.

'Then stop organising my work.'

'I'll do that the day I stop organising your finances.' Ingham's voice was silky. 'You seem to forget who pays the bills around here.'

'The mill pays for itself. Or it would if you'd leave me alone.' Archer was trembling with rage. Beth could see his hands clamped into two fists and guessed he was having difficulty in preventing himself from lashing out at the older man. Ingham said something else in a goading undertone, which she could not catch, before he turned away, and Archer's knuckles whitened into bone. He swore lamentably.

Ingham said, mildly: 'Someday someone is going to close that foul mouth of yours, my son.'

'Then it will take someone better than

you,' retorted Archer.

'Let's not brawl in front of Beth,' said Ingham, throwing her a wry smile. 'I'm sure she must find it most distasteful.' He sighed. 'Fathers and sons, my dear. A difficult relationship. I sometimes feel they had the correct idea in the Middle Ages, when they sent their offspring away to be trained and educated in somebody else's castle.'

Beth's lips curved slightly. Perhaps he was right at that, she thought, remembering her own father and Tom. T.J., too, cut down his son at each and every opportunity. But if T.J. was a blunt axe, hacking roughly, then Ingham was a rapier, thrusting to the bone. Both were ruthlessly efficient.

She said: 'How is Sebbie?' Sebastian, the son of Ingham's second wife and stepbrother to Archer. Aged thirteen, he spent his time in boarding-schools and most of his holidays abroad.

'Fine,' said Ingham. He smiled. 'I see you take my point. He's in Switzerland this summer.' He glanced towards Archer. 'I never repeat my mistakes.'

After Ingham had departed, Archer went across to the old stable and brought out the wooden boards used as tabletops at the various village functions. Shaking off Beth's attempts to help him, he propped them, one by one, against the outer wall.

'I'm surprised you trust yourself to me, alone,' he said, with a glint. 'Aren't you afraid I might fling myself on you and bite?'

Beth did not answer.

He slapped another board against the wall. 'What noble works will you be doing at the bazaar?'

'The children's refreshments.'

'That's nice. Just up your street. Lemonade and fairycakes.'

'If you say so.'

'Is Tom going with you, to hold your hand?'

'The same old Archer,' snapped Beth, stung into retaliation. 'Spiteful as ever.'

He grinned. 'Did you expect me suddenly to sprout wings?' Satisfied now that he had provoked some reaction from her, he turned once more to his task and stacked the boards neatly in the rear of the Land-Rover. That done, he stood waiting for Beth to move. When she did not, he said, rudely: 'What are you hanging about for? Christmas?'

'The trestles. Mrs Waterhouse said something about iron trestles . . . We're not going to get very far on those, are we?' said Beth acidly, again goaded into reprisal, nodding at the table-tops.

Archer looked a little sheepish. 'Yes, of course. I forgot. They're in the other shed.' Leaving Beth, he went over to a dilapidated building on the other side of the stable and heaved open the broken door which promptly swung to on him, and she could hear him cursing as he wrestled it open again with one of the heavy iron trestles in his arms. Reluctantly she went across to hold wide the door. They were so close that he brushed her with his bare arm as he went past and, for a moment, his eyes were staring straight down into hers. She saw a spark of amused malice in their depths.

'Breathe in,' he said. 'And give me a bit of room.'

Finding a large stone, Beth propped the door open and stood well back. That, too, seemed to afford him a certain amount of twisted amusement.

He pushed the last of the trestles into the back of the Land-Rover. 'There you are,' he said. 'All loaded. And with as little contamination as possible . . . So now you'd better run back to Tom, hadn't you?'

It wasn't until Beth had started the engine and drawn away that she remembered her mother's flour. Well, it would have to wait; she wasn't going back for it, Reuben could collect it in the morning. She was never going to speak with Archer again, if she could help it. But she was very conscious that he was standing staring after her, his eyes bright and sardonic under the afternoon sun.

6

'Wouldn't you just know it!' said Marjorie Channing in exasperation the next morning, surveying her eldest daughter across the otherwise empty kitchen. 'Here I am, rushed off my feet with all the catering to do for the Women's Fellowship, and everyone is suddenly spirited away.' The dishes on the dresser were still protesting faintly from the slam of the back door which had accompanied the retreat of Lucy from the family hive.

'You'd have thought Violet Pettifer would at least have had the grace to let me know she wasn't coming to help me,' grumbled Marjorie, glancing once more at the clock. 'Eleven thirty. She won't arrive now, she's due at the Village Hall to sort out the song books ... Glory be!' She threw up her hands in a flurry of flour. 'I've still got the key to the book cupboard: she was to have collected it from me this morning. Beth, you'd better take it along to her and see what's happened. Tell her I'll pick her up at the usual time this afternoon, if she's still going to the meeting.' Marjorie wiped her hands on a cloth and fished a key from a drawer in the dresser. She held it towards Beth. 'There. Don't be long, I need you here . . . Though heaven knows what transport you'll find; the truck's at the market today and Pace has the Land-Rover, and — '

'That's all right,' cut in Beth, rescuing a batch of scones from the oven. 'I'll walk. It takes less than twenty minutes by the field path and I'll be glad of a breath of fresh air.' She glanced out at the sunshine. 'Tom's not been in for coffee, so I imagine he must be up to his eyes in work as well. I'll make him a flask and drop it off as I go by.' She had seen nothing of her brother that morning. When she had arrived downstairs just before seven, the oasts had already been claiming him since dawn.

The hop-picking machine had been muscled into operation again. She could hear its heavy rumbling before she turned the corner of the yard to walk across to the shed that housed it. Three women were sitting at the end of the conveyor-belt, a short way inside the door, sorting stray leaves and fragments of bine from the stripped hops, which were passing from the belt into sacks beside them. Beth merely raised her hand in greeting, finding speech almost impossible through the din. Reuben Colley evidently experienced no such difficulty and was bellowing hoarsely at some foreign students at the other end of the long shed.

One of the women, guessing Beth was looking for her brother, jabbed a finger in the direction of the oasts and, turning, Beth stepped back through the doorway of the shed and out into the sunlight once more. Thick yellowish smoke was coming from the cowl of the second oast and from cracks around the closed shutters halfway up the dark brickwork of the kiln and a fumigatory smell of sulphur hung on the air. Beth could see her brother standing on the open gallery that fronted the drying-floor, heaving sacks of fresh hops off the elevator belt as fast as the young, fair-haired lad below could drag them across from the end of the hop-picking machine and feed them up to him. Tom then stacked them along the wooden partition behind him, ready for emptying on to the drying-floor of the oast at the next firing. He looked dirty and hot and streaked with sweat.

Running lightly up the short flight of splintery stairs that led to the upper regions, Beth walked across the slatted floor to her brother.

'Liquid refreshment,' she said with a smile, holding out the flask. 'Can you take a break?'

'Thanks,' he said, accepting it from her hand. 'I think I can spare five minutes.' He leaned forward and called down to the fair-haired worker below him: 'Five minutes, Andy. Okay?' The young man broke off his task with obvious relief and went to lean against one of the gallery support-posts.

'How is it going?' asked Beth, eyeing the tractor and trailer full of cut hop-bines that had just turned into the yard and pulled up in front of the picking-shed.

'Pretty fair,' replied Tom. He rested a shoulder on the partition which separated them from the dried hops and the hop-press and poured himself a cup of coffee. 'We should catch up on things by tomorrow, if the damned machine doesn't break down again.'

'Any chance of you coming for a walk with me? I've an errand to do at Violet Pettifer's.'

'God, no. I feel guilty about stopping to swallow this.' Tom gestured with the plastic cup from the flask. 'Those lads have worked like slaves. Reuben, too. He's been a real trump. I couldn't have managed without him.'

'I heard him cracking the whip,' said Beth dryly.

'No, really. They've all been first-class.'

'They're paid overtime, which is what they want,' said Beth. 'And I'll bet they have their scheduled breaks, too, which is more than you're allowing yourself. You'll crack up at this rate.' She eyed him soberly. 'You don't have to prove that you're as good as T.J., you know.'

'Don't I?' His tone was bleak.

'No. It's enough to do the best you can.'

He answered with a short bark of derision, but his arm came up to link loosely about her neck and they remained together for a few silent moments watching the activity in the yard.

Two student-workers in green protective clothing were standing on the trailer by the machine-shed, engaged in fastening the hop-bines, singly, to hang like long green hanks of hair, in the gripper-like hooks of a high, slowly moving belt which circled through the open end of the machine-shed, fed its load, one by one, into the hop-picking machine and returned, empty, through a gap in the shed wall, ready to be reprimed by the waiting acolytes with more hop-bines. Above the rumble of the moving machinery and the chatter of foreign accents, Beth could hear the nearer muted roar of the powerful burner just below her, to her right, and situated under the drying-floor of the number two kiln, and she could picture its fierce jet of flame, like some demented rocket blasting through space. The acrid smell of the sulphur it was burning was heavy in her nostrils.

'Will you be in for a midday meal?' she enquired at last.

'No,' said Tom abstractedly, moving to the edge of the platform and signalling to his helper to restart the elevator. 'Don't wait for me; I'll grab a sandwich when I can.' He was already bending forward to grasp the first sack on its upward journey before Beth reached the bottom of the wooden steps.

Thankful to be in clear sunshine again, away from the close, oven-like heat, the noise and the fumes, Beth — with none of Tom's frantic desire to prove anything to anybody — wound a leisurely way along the track that led to Violet Pettifer's cottage. Past the first hopfield, already shorn of its dark, hanging vines, past the second, and larger, hopfield, where she could see another tractor and trailer at work, employed in cutting down the large-leaved bines, the green-enveloped figures of the workers unrecognisable under their protective hoods. All the paths and tracks ran ankle deep in grey dust, the legacy of the long spell of hot weather on the chalklands, and ready at the first rainstorm to turn into a hideous foot-and-tyre-slipping slurry. Beth could sympathise with Tom's wish to have all safely gathered in while the weather held. She eyed the sky anxiously: not a cloud in sight, but the blue bowl hung heavily, shimmering away to a ruddy haze in the distance.

Turning sharply to her left, opposite the experimental wheatfield with its flower-studded headlands and dividing sterile strip, she continued her way along the cart-track that flanked the rear of the Mumford place, now silent under the sun, and climbed the stile that led the field path in the direction of the village of Otley Ash. The grass had been cut as hay in June, but was ready for a second shearing. A few dandelion-seeds drifted across in front of her, ethereal, silver-white in the sunlight, and slowly, delicately, rising towards the east where, among the tired green, gorse spat occasional golden sparks.

Violet's back gate opened directly on to the grassy footpath and stood ajar and one step through it took Beth into a neat garden ablaze with dahlias. No one was about. Dewey's hedge-clippings were piled in a corner by the vegetable plot and the wheelbarrow was upended beside them. Beth walked down the flagged path and knocked briskly on the back door. Nobody came. Beth tried again, then, after waiting for a minute or two, took herself round to the front door and gave that a hammering. Still no one came. Violet, apparently, was out. Beth frowned. The milk was on the doorstep; not, in itself, anything to cause alarm, but at least unusual at that hour. And the porch lamp was still on, burning wanly through the sunshine.

Stepping backwards, Beth studied the house, all tranquil, all quiet, the white weatherboarding eye-dazzling under the bright noon light; the curtains neatly drawn together. The curtains closed? At midday? Again she frowned, beginning to feel a sense of unease. Violet was one of the world's early risers — a proverbial lark to catch the unwary worm.

Leaving the porch, Beth ran round to the rear of the cottage again. Here, too, the curtains were still tightly closed. She pressed the door-latch and found it opened beneath her hand.

'Violet?' she called softly. Then, receiving no reply, more loudly. There was a strange, unpleasant smell in the house which Beth could not identify, but which caught in her throat and made her want to retch. Slowly she moved through the hall to the kitchen. Here the sickly smell was stronger, a sort of cloying, stomach-churning stench. Violet had evidently eaten supper for a few congealed scraps were on a plate at one end of the table and the evening paper was propped against the cold teapot. A teacup lay shattered on the floor, its contents sprayed stickily across the tiles. Jars of homemade plum jam stood on the window-sill, minus their seals, as if they had been left to cool and then forgotten. On the stove was a frying-pan, and a dish of mushrooms prepared for cooking. Beth stared at it for a second or two before going to the kitchen door and out into the hall once more. She found Violet at her next attempt, lying contorted on the floor between the washbasin and the bath. She was dead, and she was cold, and she had obviously been sick, for a trail of vomit marked a slimed trail across the carpet.

Beth had a strong stomach and the true countrywoman's stolid attitude to the physical facts of death, but she was unable to remain any longer in that terrible little room, with all its grisly evidence of a tormented dying. For the rest of her life she would be unable to forget Violet's horrifically twisted face and the pathetic hands drawn by agony into claws.

The cottage was not on the telephone and Beth, keeping her head, made for the local doctor, Benson, a friend of the family who lived on the near side of the village.

'Beth Channing! And what brings you here with a face like a duck's egg?' Richard Benson rallied her. Apart from

T..J, with his severe and recurring bouts of gout, the Channings were hale and hearty and quite disgustingly healthy.

Beth gasped forth her story.

'I think she's accidentally poisoned herself,' she finished, through chattering teeth. 'With mushrooms. She'd already eaten some, there were a few pieces on her plate, and another dishful on the stove, and she'd been sick — '

The doctor took her arm to steady her. 'I don't believe we've lost anyone around here from mushroom poisoning yet,' he said.

'Toadstools, then. She must have eaten toadstools by mistake.' Beth's voice was rising and she was shaking all over. 'Something really deadly, like Fly Agaric — or Death Caps.'

Richard Benson said quietly: 'We'll see.' He didn't doubt Beth's statement that Violet was dead. The girl was too level-headed to make any mistake in that direction. How was another matter. 'Come along. I'll just phone Jim Tate.'

She stared at him.

'The police have to be there, Beth. In

any case of unexpected sudden death, the police have to be informed.' He glanced sideways at her. 'If things are as you say, there'll have to be a post-mortem, you know. To find out exactly how she died.'

Beth nodded and swallowed.

'Do you feel able to come back there with me? It would help. You can answer my questions as you go along and be on the scene when Tate arrives.'

Again Beth nodded. There was no point in refusing. At some stage or another she would have to give her story, so it might as well be now. She found she was still shaking.

Later Tom, having heard Beth's theory about the toadstools, seemed inclined to believe that he might be at least partly to blame for Violet's accident.

'If I hadn't told her to go gathering mushrooms in Larks' Meadow, she might be alive now,' he said bitterly, halting to snatch a hurried word with Beth as he crossed the yard during the middle of the following afternoon.

'That's nonsense,' retorted Beth smartly. 'You don't know that she took your advice and, if she did, they really are mushrooms that grow there, not poisonous toadstools. She must have picked those from somewhere else: in the woods, I imagine.' But she had no opportunity to discuss matters further, for T.J. arrived at that moment, breathing fire and bellowing imprecations round the yard.

'Damn you, Tom,' he shouted, catching sight of his son with Beth. 'Move yourself! That burner's misfiring again. Can't you do anything properly? I could manage this lot with one hand tied behind my back when I was your age.' His scowl deepened. 'If you weren't such a lazy dog yourself, the men would work harder.'

Tom turned on his heel and walked away in the direction of the oast-houses. He had said nothing, but had gone very white, and there was a strained look about his eyes that Beth didn't like. Hurriedly she helped her father into the house and, after a second's hesitation, ran upstairs to collect a couple of towels before going outside once more to find her brother.

She unearthed him up at the hop-press,

filling one of the enormous sacks that stood over a head taller than she did, with dried hops raked from the kilns, ready for one of the breweries. Beth waited until he'd completed his task and until Reuben and Andy, on the ground area below, had removed the sack from the opening under the press. Then she grasped his arm. 'Come on,' she said, 'we're playing hooky.'

He stared at her in amazement. 'I can't. There's too much to do. You heard the old man just now . . . '

'Yes. Run here, run there — I haven't noticed him doing much running lately.'

'Only to fat,' said Tom burningly. Then, catching her eye, he burst out laughing.

'That's better,' said Beth. 'So, we're agreed. We don't have to dance to his tune.'

'Ridiculous, isn't it? But he paralyses the brain.'

'Not mine, he doesn't,' said Beth stoutly. 'Come along, brother, best foot forward. I've sent Jordan to collect the horses.'

'Horses? We're going riding?' He

caught sight of the towels under her arm. 'And swimming?' His eyes came up to hers. 'You must be out of your head. I can't spare the time to go gallivanting off to the lakes, if that's what you had in mind.'

'Not the lakes. Ashpool, where we used to swim as kids. That part of the river's fine again since the new sluice has been put in, and the water's as clear as glass; I checked there a couple of days ago.' She took his arm coaxingly. 'Come on. It's like Vulcan's forge up here, the sweat's absolutely dripping off you. Come and cool off before you explode. Reuben will be only too pleased to take charge and lord it over everyone for an hour or so.' She flashed him a mischievous smile. 'Let's see if I can still beat you hollow under water.'

His mouth curved as he capitulated. 'You just might at that, until I get my second wind. Archer was . . . ' His voice tailed off. Archer had always beaten them both hollow. He said, quickly: 'Remember Esther's dictum?'

Beth gave a peal of laughter. 'Yes. After

one of the school swimming galas. She said I might not be swift, but at least I was sturdy . . . I was very hurt.'

'She meant it as a compliment. She admired your stamina.'

'I know.' Beth followed her brother down the wooden steps and across to the waiting horses. 'Funny how Esther's remarks always have a sting in the tail. Rather like Ingham's. I'm never really sure what he is thinking, either.'

'Oh, old Ingham's all right.' Tom held her horse while she mounted. He paused for a few rapid words with Reuben, then he, too, was mounting and pressing his knees into his horse's flanks and urging the animal forward, along the track that led in the direction of the river, leaving Beth to canter into position beside him . . .

But it was well over the hour they had allotted themselves before they left the river to head for home again.

Tom trailed Beth along the bank, his shirt slung over one bare shoulder. 'Not so fast,' he protested lazily, staying her hand as she started to untie the horses.

'I'm in no hurry to get back.'

'Then you've changed your song from an hour ago.'

'I've decided I might as well be hanged for a sheep as for a lamb.' He took the reins from her. 'Anyhow, we must do this again sometime.' There came to him a sudden mental flash of his sister, all honey-gold and lithe and lovely, cleaving the water with firm, strong strokes and rising, laughing, at his elbow, in a shower of diamond drops, her breasts taut-tipped with cold. He pulled himself up sharply. 'On second thoughts, perhaps it's not such a good idea.'

'Why not?'

For a moment his eyes held hers, clear grey against grey, then, with a wicked little laugh, he said: 'Don't you know?' He tossed his towel at her. 'Is Jeff back yet?'

'No, he's due home tomorrow.' She answered without much apparent interest in the fact.

'There speaks a lovelorn lady,' said Tom. He searched her face, still smiling. 'Don't get me wrong, sis, I like the guy, but what do you see in him?'

Beth wrinkled her nose. 'He's sweet. He's good-tempered, and kind, and reliable.'

'So am I.'

'Granted . . . ' She grinned. 'But Jeff does have certain vital attributes which you can't offer me.' She threw his towel back at him. 'Anyhow, seeing that you are being prodigal with time, we'll circle wide and take in the village and collect an evening paper.'

There was nothing in it about Violet Pettifer's death, although they had hardly expected there would be: the world of Otley Ash was small and insular and the local paper with its more parochial news did not come out for another two days.

Trotting along the lane from the village a few minutes later, they came up behind Lucy and the Mumford boy, who were walking dispiritedly along towards the farm. Unless he had developed a permanent list to starboard, there was a blister on Georgie's heel. Both Tom and Beth dismounted and Tom helped the youngster on to his horse and carried on alongside holding the leading rein, while

Beth fell into step with her sister on his other side.

'What are you two doing here?' asked Tom.

'What do you think!' retorted Lucy with bitterness. 'This has been the second rotten rehearsal I've held today.'

Tom glanced down at the fair head, amused. 'How do you like the choir?'

'Gagged,' returned Lucy, pithily.

'That bad?'

'They're diabolical. The rector must be tone-deaf if he imagines they can sing.'

'Never mind, I'm sure you'll work marvels.'

'I'll bally well have to, won't I? The festival is tomorrow.' She treated him to a sour scowl.

'Cheer up. You have the Reads' shindig to look forward to, tonight.'

Lucy brightened. 'Yes. May I take Dancer, Beth, and ride on ahead? I want to wash my hair.' Without waiting for an answer she swung herself to the saddle, but her intended fast exit was blocked by Richard Benson's car which curved in to a halt in front of them. The doctor leaned from the open window.

'Beth . . . I thought you'd like to know — we've had the results from the post-mortem on Violet Pettifer. Sorry I bawled you out, yesterday; you were right, she did die from eating toadstools. *Amanita phalloides*, to be precise — Death Caps. The analysis of the uneaten food on the dish was the same. The fungus she had gathered was one of the most deadly of the *Amanitas* — the Death Cap. An appalling accident. It shows one can't be too careful when dealing with fungi . . . ' He thrust his head further from the window and addressed himself to Georgie. 'Let that be a warning to you, young Georgie, to you and that little sister of yours — don't eat anything you find in the hedgerows. It could be fatal.' His eyes slewed back to Beth. 'Of course, there'll have to be an inquest, but it should be a mere formality. Nothing for you to worry about.' And he was gone.

Tom and Beth looked at each other.

'So it really was the mushrooms — or

toadstools, rather — that killed her?' said Tom slowly.

'I still don't see how she could have made that mistake,' Lucy protested. 'Not unless she was thick as a brick.'

'Death Caps can resemble mushrooms very closely,' said Beth. 'Especially when the fungus is young.' She turned to her brother. 'But she couldn't have picked her batch from Larks' Meadow, Tom, if that's what you're afraid of. Death Caps have never grown there.'

'Anyhow,' put in Georgie decidedly, from his perch on Tom's horse, 'she didn't pick them herself. They were a present.'

All eyes swivelled to his.

'What did you say?' said Tom at last, faintly.

'I said that they were a present to her.'

'Who told you?'

'She did. I took her some empty jam-jars the day before yesterday, after tea, and she showed me the basketful of mushrooms. A lovely present, she said.'

'Georgie Mumford!' Lucy looked at

him severely. 'If this is another of your tall stories — '

'It ain't a tall story. I'm just telling you what she said.'

Lucy tossed her hair. 'You can't take any notice of what he says, Tom. He's a born liar.'

'I ain't.'

'You are. You'd do anything for a bit of limelight.'

'Nuts to you, Goosey Lucy. Go wash your hair and shrink your head,' retorted Georgie valiantly and had the satisfaction of seeing Lucy wheel and ride angrily away from them.

For a few seconds nobody said anything, then Tom swung round once more to the boy. 'Georgie — Violet said she had the mushrooms given to her, you say? By whom?'

'I don't know,' replied Georgie in disgust, tiring of the subject. 'Old Petticoats didn't tell me . . . Can't we get along home now?'

'Yes, of course,' nodded Beth. She turned to her brother. 'I'll see Georgie to his door and attend to the horses, if you want to return to the oast.' She eyed him anxiously. His face had taken on that grey look of strain again and his voice sounded thin, like stretched wire. She said: 'At least you know now that it was nothing you said which sent Violet out to pick those toadstools.'

'No.' He stood staring unseeingly at the hawkbits that gilded the roadside.

'I suppose we could mention it to Jim Tate.'

'Mention what? Georgie's so-called information?' He frowned. 'I don't suppose the child really knows anything. Anyhow, even if what he said is true, it must have been an accident — no one would have done such a thing on purpose.'

'Unless it was some kind of nasty practical joke that misfired.'

'No!' Tom stared at her in shock. 'Nobody would be so stupid. It's sure to have been a genuine mistake. Someone trying to be kind and picking the wrong things.'

'Then why haven't they come forward and explained?'

'Panic? Fear? Or perhaps they haven't heard about Vi's death yet.' He shook his head at her expression of disbelief. 'That's possible, Beth. Give them time.' He squeezed her shoulder as he moved, and she watched him stride away from her across the corner of the field towards the oast-houses. And work there swallowed him for the rest of the day and well into the dusk.

It was nine-thirty before she heard him enter the farmhouse and go upstairs and the evening meal had long been cleared away. She waited for twenty minutes and then went to look for him. He was in his room, sitting on the edge of the bed, his hands dangling between his knees and his eyes just staring into space.

Beth crossed to his side. 'Don't you want anything to eat? Mother worries when you miss meals.'

'Keeps me trim,' he said dully, turning to her a face almost as white and exhausted as the crushed chalk which liberally decorated the floor. Against his pallor the unshaven stubble on his cheeks showed darkly.

'It's a mess in here,' said Beth, brushing a fine film of dust from the chest beside him. 'Where did all this chalk come from?' She bent and gathered up a shirt and a pair of trousers which had been bundled in the corner by the bedhead.

'Leave those,' said Tom.

Beth straightened and shook out the trousers she was holding. They, too, were covered in chalkdust. 'If I leave them any longer they'll walk out of the room by themselves,' she replied tartly. 'I'll take them downstairs to be cleaned.'

Tom watched her tuck the offending garments under her arm and caught her to him as she passed. 'Fancy going down to the Bell, Beth? Drown our sorrows?'

'Amen to that.'

'I can afford to stand you half a pint.' He flashed her a shadow of his old grin.

'Good. And I hope you intend to have a shave before you go; you look ready to rob a bank.' She extricated herself from the circle of his arm and walked to the door. 'Did you see Lucy when she left? She looked very pretty . . . I can't say I'm happy about this party at the Reads', though. Lucy is too young to cope with Archer if he tries anything, and heaven knows how far he'd go just to spite us, but — ' Beth pulled a face ' — Mother trusts Archer, she says, so . . . '

'If he lays a finger on Lucy he won't want another girl for as long as he lives,' growled Tom. 'That I promise you.' And Beth left him tracing a toe in the chalkdust on the floor, his eyes staring blindly past the ghostly flower faces beyond his window and out, once more, into space.

7

The powerful sports car gunned up the last stretch of hill and snarled to a halt beside Esther's gate, blocked at the moment by an untidy pile of fruit-picking ladders. Archer Read climbed out.

'Who the hell left this lot here? Move them.' His temper was not improved by the earliness of the morning, nor by the lateness of the party he'd endured the night before. It was improved still less when he strode around the old pick-up truck which had been delivering the ladders and found himself face to face with Tom Channing.

'Get your bloody stuff away from the entrance, Channing,' he shouted. 'Shift it!'

Tom, who had been going to do just that, folded his arms. 'Shift it yourself,' he said.

Archer moved threateningly. 'Do I have to make you?'

'You could try,' said Tom smoothly, not stirring a muscle.

'Tom!'

Archer spun, realising for the first time that the man in front of him was not alone. Beth stood by the orchard gate.

Ignoring him, she ran forward and, grasping a couple of the ladders, began to tow them over to the fence. They were heavy and she made slow progress. Archer strode towards her. For a heartbeat, as he reached her side, he saw a faint shadow leap across her eyes, gone as soon as identified. A flicker of fear. It did not help his temper. He took the ladders from her and hurled them down by the fence.

He said: 'Do you always let your women do your work for you, Channing?'

Beth said coolly: 'I can manage.'

'I dare say you can,' snapped Archer, 'but I can't wait all day.' Catching the small sardonic lift of her brows, he felt a sudden violent urge to hurt her — and not just with words, trading insults whenever their paths happened to cross, but really, physically, savagely, to hurt her. He recognised how primitive were his emotions. He wanted to fling himself at her, to take her down and force himself on her, and into her, and hear her beg . . . Both power and pleasure. His eyes greened.

He regarded her tauntingly, with a face that was a little flushed, and said: 'Your young sister enjoyed herself last night.'

Beth's eyes swept up to his. Again there was the slight fearful quiver in their depths, but she answered steadily enough. 'Yes, she did, she's sleeping it off this morning.' She watched Tom shoulder a ladder across to the orchard. 'I understand the youngsters were viewing some foreign films?'

He smiled. 'Skinflicks, as Ingham so quaintly calls them.'

'You mean you were running blue movies,' ground out Tom at his elbow.

'Black and white, actually,' drawled Archer, in a goading tone. 'Although I fail to see what business it is of yours, Channing. Lucy had no complaints.'

'Why, — you — ' Tom broke off with an oath. 'One day, so help me, Archer Read, I'm going to fix you for good.'

'With or without a handicap?'

Beth grabbed Tom's swinging arm. 'Stop it, Tom, he's not worth it.'

'Oh, I'm worth it, sweetie, make no mistake about that. Any time big brother chooses.'

'He's only needling you, Tom,' cried Beth.

'When I do some needling, it won't be with Dog Tom,' retorted Archer.

But Beth was already urging her brother towards their truck and they had raced away, taking the corner far too fast, long before Archer had made any move to slide back into his car and carry on up the drive to the house.

Esther was standing outside her door. 'Was that the Channings with the ladders they promised me? The fruit-pickers are coming this morning.' She shaded her eyes with her hand. The sun burned through the morning cloud, dazzlingly. 'I was just finishing breakfast.'

'I trust you steered clear of mushrooms!'

Esther looked as if he had struck her. She shot fiercely: 'And what exactly is

137

that supposed to mean?'

'Nothing,' Archer said, taken aback. 'Nothing. It was a joke, that's all.'

'In very poor taste, then.'

He stared at her in helpless silence.

'You find Violet Pettifer's death funny?' she demanded.

'No. Sorry, Esther. But you know my irreverent tongue . . . '

Esther stepped forward, her dress shaking moisture from the fuchsia bush at her side. The vivid, ballerina-skirted flowers danced. Mist was smoking up from the damp grass and coiling away in the valley. Higher, the slopes of the hillside were already clear.

She scowled. 'Well, Archer, two visits from you in one week. To what do I owe my sudden popularity?'

'Your gentle speech and sweet personality.'

Her laugh was short. 'What do you want?'

'What makes you think I want something?'

'People usually do.'

'You're right, of course.' His eyes roved

138

past the terrace and came to rest near the cellar door. 'Dewey mentioned that you'd cut down the old elder-tree.'

'Yes. I grew tired of it attacking my drains.'

'I wondered if I might beg some of the wood for my mill? For cogs. There are several parts of the machinery I have to renew myself and mature elderwood is even better than hornbeam for my purpose.'

'Help yourself.' She indicated a pile of branches and thick root-stock and watched as he chose those pieces he thought would be most suitable, deftly cutting away the newer growth with a small saw he had taken from the car and carving deeply from the ancient trunk.

'An odd tree, the elder,' he mused, staring at the pale wood under his hand. 'When young, its branches are composed almost entirely of pith — one of the lightest stuffs known to man, yet the wood from the mature trunk is as hard as ebony.' He slipped his acquisitions into a sack and stood it on the passenger-seat of his car, where it perched precariously, an incongruous travelling companion. He swung round. 'Oh, there was one other thing. The corn dollies. May I have first pick before the village maul them over at the bazaar? Melinda is keen on that sort of thing and I promised to ask you if we could have two or three nice ones for her flat.'

'You'll have to wait until I get them back from the church, every last one of them is there at the moment.'

'In the church? But it's not Harvest Festival till the end of the month.'

She smiled. 'The rector's gone all folksy on us; he wanted decorations for the concert tonight, anything suitably rustic. I let him have all the corn dollies and my plaques and umpteen other bits and pieces. I'm surprised you weren't asked to contribute a bag of flour.' Her tone was dry. 'But I believe Marjorie Channing is baking fancy bread. Anyhow, everything will be returned to be sold on the stalls, so you can have your choice then . . . Unless you'd like me to weave you some more?'

'No, I'll wait. It's not that important.'

Esther paused, head on one side. 'Are you still thick with Melinda, then?'

'Depends what you mean by 'thick'.'

'You know what I mean.' She eyed him darkly.

He grinned satanically. 'Am I having it off with Melinda? Is that what you are trying to ask? Well, the answer is maybe, and maybe not . . . Who wants to know? Tom?'

'Tom would hardly get me to do his dirty work for him.'

'No. And Tom doesn't really care about Melinda, anyway, does he? His interests lie closer to home.'

Esther shrugged. 'I should watch my mouth if I were you.'

'But you're not me, are you, Esther dear?'

The old woman flung him a sharp glance. 'I take it that you are going to the church tonight, to the music festival?'

'Yes,' he agreed.

'And that's a sight we don't often see.'

'Oh, I don't know . . . ' His tone was flippant. 'I try to attend all the christenings, marryings and funerals.'

'Yes, and that's just the order in which things would be arranged by you, Archer,' she countered acidly.

The dark, beautifully-shaped brows rose at her and she gave a hoarse chuckle.

'Gossip, lad. If you cough in the morning, here, by evening they'll have you dead with galloping consumption.' She paused. 'Is Melinda going to the festival?'

'No, it's not her cup of tea.'

'Then Ingham won't be going either.' There was something about the flat statement that brought his eyes round to hers. Her bright marigold stare was upon him, sardonic and very slightly malevolent. And without any shadow of doubt he knew she had guessed about Ingham and Melinda.

'Somewhere in your ancestry, Esther Deauville, there was a witch,' he said softly. 'No, Ingham won't be going to the concert. Ingham is supervising the arrangements for the bun-fight afterwards at the house. The diva's farewell.' His eyes were mocking. But he had fallen, very neatly, into her trap.

'Then you'll be going alone?' She stared at the cowls of the oast-houses rising through the last wreaths of mist in the valley. 'You can pick me up.'

His cheek-muscles twitched slightly. Too late he had seen where she was heading. He bowed slightly. 'It would be a pleasure, dear Esther.'

'I don't know about that.' Her voice was dry. 'But it'd certainly save my feet.'

'In my sports car?'

'Well, lad, I'm not fixing to go in your tractor and trailer, if that's what you're thinking. I'm sure I can be as sporty as the next woman.'

'I'm sure you can.' He almost, but not quite, hid a grin.

'And you can take that look off your face, Archer Read, you're not such a sharp apple. I know what you get up to, don't think that I don't. And I can tell you right now that I don't approve. Having too many girls is like having too much wine — it leaves you bleary-eyed and fuddle-headed.'

'I expect you're right,' he said humbly. 'Tonight shall be devoted entirely to you.'

'Hmmmph,' she said. 'Let's hope the shock isn't too great for your system.' She watched his smile come and go, like sunshine flickering over water, and noticed that it did not touch his eyes. For all his carryings-on, as she put it to herself, he was not happy.

'I'll pick you up at six-thirty,' he said. And it was only a little later than the appointed hour when they drew alongside the lychgate that evening. It seemed that the whole village was on its way up the cobbled path to the church.

'Don't rush me,' grumbled Esther, clinging tightly to Archer's arm. 'We've plenty of time; I want to speak to someone.' She had spotted the Channing sisters with their mother and Jeff Newton, walking several paces behind them. 'Beth!' she called imperiously. And, when Esther called, people listened. Beth moved reluctantly towards her, urged forward on either side by those around her. Jeff had no choice but to continue escorting Marjorie and Lucy into church.

Esther grabbed Beth's arm with her

free hand and held it like a limpet. 'Where's Tom?'

'He was unable to come,' said Beth. 'There was a crisis at the oasts and he had to stay behind to sort it out.'

'Pity. I wanted to ask him to have a look at my portable television. It's on the blink, and I like to watch it when I'm in bed.'

'I can think of better things to do in bed,' murmured Archer, trying to disengage his arm from her fingers which were digging into him like claws.

'I'll mention it to Tom,' said Beth, also trying to wrest herself free. 'I must go, Esther, Jeff will wonder where I am.'

'Jeff knows where you are,' replied Esther tartly. 'You're helping me into church.' She leaned upon them both heavily and for the first time that evening they recalled her age. Silently they assisted her towards the west door where, on the old flintwork corner above their heads, a stone gargoyle smirked timelessly. Its small devil's smile reminded Beth and Archer irresistibly of the woman between them.

Inside the church, Esther manoeuvred her two captives in front of her, still holding tightly to their arms, and guided them into a pew as if they were two dim-witted children. 'You can help me out again, after the concert,' she whispered, seating herself at the end of the bench and blocking all escape. She bowed her head.

'You planned this,' said Beth in a furious undertone to Archer.

'Don't flatter yourself,' he retorted. 'I was looking forward to an enjoyable evening.' And he turned his shoulder on her.

'Sit down,' hissed Esther. 'Everyone's looking at you.'

Beth and Archer subsided on the seat, stiffly and apart.

Esther dug a sharp elbow in his ribs. 'Move up,' she commanded. 'Mrs Mumford wants to sit down.'

There was no help for it; they were well and truly trapped.

Beth heard little of the concert. She was conscious of the silver notes of the famous singer, rising and falling around the vaulted building, conscious, too, of Lucy haloed at the organ, a small angel in a pool of coloured light, but conscious most of all of the dark figure sitting at her side, his eyes ranging the church. Archer, too, was not attending to the music.

She watched him covertly from beneath her lashes. He appeared to be making a great show of examining the decorations, and she had to admit that they were very fine; Mrs Waterhouse and her helpers had done a sterling job. Swags of hand-woven cloth hid the grey stone walls and tumbled over the edges of the pulpit, home-crafted wicker baskets held fruit and flowers, and a variety of other craftwork decorated the wide window-sills. Beth could see the corn dollies made by Esther and the children everywhere she glanced, the ribbon bows that tied them gay against the gloom, reds and blues and greens and golds, like exotic butterflies arrested in flight. And over all, obliterating the usual odours of old hymn-books, polish and candlewax, floated the thick, soporific smell of hops. A crane-fly paddled its long legs in the corner of the window above her head.

Turning, Beth surprised Esther's gaze on Archer, her orange-gold eyes bright and oddly malicious. Aware that Beth was now staring at her, the old woman tipped her head to one side and began again to listen devotedly to the music . . .

And the festival concert flowed steadily on towards its close.

Gradually the westering sun dipped to catch Georgie Mumford's hair in a shaft of light, changing its red into a flaming aureole. While the same lengthening rays spilled through the glass of Esther's plaques and sent the colours glittering across the choir like jewels on the snowy surplices; emerald and topaz, amethyst and ruby, and shades of sapphire, rivalling the burning lozenges from the stained-glass windows. Floating motes of dust danced golden in the last sunshine, until, suddenly, the brightness had drained away and the church was full of soft shadows and dusky shapes. And the lamps came on.

Outside, ghost moths were fluttering among the white campions on the overgrown gravestones when Esther, still clinging to her two unwilling supporters, lingered to speak to Lucy.

'Congratulations,' she said. 'To you and to the choir. They were a credit to you, girl. And you were beautiful.'

'She was, wasn't she?' laughed Archer.

Esther shot him a sour look. 'I'm surprised you heard a word, you seemed more interested in the décor than the diva . . . ' She gave him a smile of pure malice. 'What were you searching for, Archer? Lavender?' Archer's dark brows snapped down, but Esther had already turned from him to Lucy. 'Who's taking you home, child?' The ranks around them were thinning. Jeff, with Marjorie Channing, was waiting patiently outside the gate.

'Mr Waterhouse,' said Lucy, tipsy with success. 'All the choir, in the mini-bus; we're having supper at the rectory.' She waved across to her mother and Jeff. 'Mr Waterhouse is seeing us home,' she carolled to them.

It was not until Beth reached the gate and found that Jeff and her mother had gone that she realised they had mistaken Lucy's excited message; they had believed that Beth, too, was on her way to the rectory.

'Never mind,' said Esther. 'Archer'll squeeze you in with me, somehow.'

'In that?' said Beth, nodding her head at the rakish lines of the two-seater sports car. 'No, thank you.' She had no intention of cuddling up to Archer at Esther's bidding. 'I'll walk.'

'Suit yourself,' said Archer. He smiled crookedly and started the engine.

Beth walked home across the field path with the Mumfords and so had no idea that, after he had delivered Esther safely to Elderwood, Archer had raced back for her.

8

'Who is that?' Marjorie Channing looked up from her baking, her arms flour to the wrists, as the sound of a powerful engine died outside. It was the morning after the concert and she was again alone in the kitchen with Beth.

'Archer Read,' said Beth in a strangled voice, from her vantage-point in front of the window that backed the sink.

'Archer?' lilted Marjorie happily, wiping her hands. 'Then don't just stand there, let him in ... Archer — how lovely to see you again!' She ran forward, eyes shining, receiving him like the prodigal son. If he had held any doubts about his welcome, they were resolved by the warmth of her greeting.

'Hello, Marjorie.' He kissed her flushed cheek. 'I've brought the stoneground flour you wanted; it was forgotten the other day.'

'That's extremely kind of you,' she said effusively.

'No need to go overboard about it,' muttered Beth, whipping soap-suds in the sink.

Marjorie flashed her an exasperated look. 'Beth, leave that and make us some coffee . . . You'll stay for coffee, Archer?'

'Don't bother on my account,' he said. 'I can see you're busy.'

'It's no bother . . . Beth!'

Unwillingly Beth walked across to switch on the electric kettle. 'It'll have to be instant,' she said ungraciously. She turned her back on them and set about clattering cups and saucers on a tray.

'I tried to have a word with you outside the church, Archer,' said Marjorie, 'but there was no opportunity. I'm so pleased that you've come to see us at long last. I was beginning to think you'd cut us out of your life for ever.'

Archer's gaze roved the kitchen. 'You haven't changed anything. This was always my favourite place.'

'Then make sure you enjoy it more often in future.'

'I will.' He watched her cross to the oven and open the door. The smell of freshly-baked bread filled the room.

Beth held out his coffee to him in silence.

'Thank you,' he said, taking the cup from her. He studied her over the rim. 'You're looking blooming ... How is Jeff?'

'Fit.' Beth ground her teeth and carried on the farce of conversation. 'And Melinda?'

'Surpassing all expectations.' His eyes mocked her.

Beth moved away. 'Mother, it's late, I have to go and feed the hens — '

'Yes, dear. Take Archer with you, I expect he'd like to see the new generator.'

'Mother, I haven't time this morning. I must feed the hens and — '

'Your father was saying, Archer,' went on Marjorie, ignoring her daughter, 'that you were thinking of setting up a small generator in the shed behind the mill. One like ours would be ideal; it's a Gresham, very compact, and T.J. is pleased with its performance ... But

Beth can tell you more about the thing than I can — can't you, Beth?'

'Perhaps some other time,' said Beth. 'I have to feed the hens and then I have to . . . ' Her voice trailed off as she caught Archer's eyes on her. They were the clear grey-green of a summer sea and were smiling down at her. The mockery had gone. So, too, had the angry dislike. He was regarding her with an odd expression — with amusement, certainly, but also with affection and — tenderness, was it? Beth felt the blood rush to her face. Her heart gave a queer little jerk and began slamming against her chest like a trip-hammer. Completely unnerved, she stuttered: 'And then I must go and feed the hens . . . feed the hens — '

Marjorie's voice cut through her paralysis. 'Beth! Wake up! What do you intend to do then?'

'Feed the hens, I shouldn't wonder,' said Archer, devils in his eyes.

Beth slid past him, went out and closed the door behind her.

Archer glanced across at Marjorie who half raised a shoulder in sympathy.

'It's hard going, lad.'

'No more than I deserve.' He smiled ruefully and placed his cup back on the table. 'Well, I'll be off, then. See you some time.' He took a step towards the door.

'It's none of my business, of course, but — '

Archer stopped and turned back to her.

' — this quarrel . . . ' Marjorie looked down at her hands. 'Surely it can have been no more than a small tiff that's grown out of all proportion, and — '

'Beth never told you?'

'No. But then Beth wouldn't; she has a mouth like a rat-trap — '

'Except where Tom's concerned.' His tone was bitter.

'I don't know about that.' Her head came up. 'I don't wish to know anything about any of it . . . ' She looked over his shoulder, out through the window. The sun caught the grey in her hair dimming its gold as if with dust. 'Tom is busy at the oast,' she said reflectively. Her eyes came back to his. 'Doubtless Beth will be in the grain shed . . . Go after her, Archer, and make your peace.'

The great barn where most of the feeding stuffs were kept was dim after the brightness of the sun outside, but Archer could hear small movements from within; the rustle of straw, the clink of metal against metal, a soft swish of sliding grain . . .

At first, intent on her task, Beth neither saw nor heard him. It was only when his shadow fell across her that she looked up and took a tiny backwards step. Recovering herself, she grabbed her bucket and made to pass him. He stayed her with his hand.

'Beth, we have to talk.'

'I have nothing to say to you.' She shook off his hold. For answer, he tore the bucket from her fingers and crashed it upon the ground.

'We talk!' he said. He slammed her back against the corn-bin so roughly that it took her breath away. Then his hands were gripping her upper arms and pinning her there, arched across the bin. The metal edge bit painfully into her spine. Naked fear flashed in her eyes.

'Archer, you're hurting me — '

His grasp slowly slackened until she could draw herself upright, and they stood face to face, although he kept his hands on her arms, a hold that was now merely detaining but which would, she guessed, tighten into a band of steel if she attempted to slip away. The familiar smell of him was in her nostrils, strangely heart-tugging, a compound of soap and his aftershave, of chrysanthemums, and newly-cut wood, and male exertion.

'Just listen,' he said, 'that's all I ask.' The flicker of fear in her eyes had cut him to the quick. 'Then, if you're still of the same mind, I promise I'll never trouble you again.'

'Go ahead,' she gritted. 'Talk. Don't say you've come to tell me you're sorry!'

'No, damn you, I haven't. Not this time. It's too late for that. I'm not sorry. I enjoyed it: it was the last bright spot in all these past months.'

She stared at him, lips parted, and he laughed softly.

'All right, my love. Just a little bit sorry then, for making you so mad — but not for loving you . . . '

'Is that what you call it?'

His hands dropped from her arms and he lifted her chin. 'Beth . . . I was drunk — '

'But not incapable.'

'No . . . ' He sighed. 'I suppose we have to go through all this, but it seems so pointless, so unimportant, such a song-and-dance about not very much. And so unlike you, Beth. So, I got drunk. I made a mistake. I forced myself on you when you quite clearly didn't want me. But none of that alters the fact that I loved you, that I wanted to marry you — I still do.'

She shook her head numbly, eyes overbright with tears. 'Do you remember anything of that night? Anything at all?'

'I've just told you — '

'Apart from my song-and-dance, as you put it?'

He frowned, struggling to recall through long past months things that had been far from clear even at the beginning.

He blinked. 'You mean those things I said about Tom?'

'About me and Tom.'

158

His feet shifted. 'I was drunk at the time — '

'So it seems — '

'And whose fault was it I'd been drinking in the first place? Answer me that. Not many men have to compete with their girl's own brother. I did.'

'That's not true.'

'You know damned well it was true. And then you tried to come over prissy with me — '

'I said 'no' that was all.'

'You chose the wrong man to say it to, then.'

'Oh, Archer, don't let's fight,' she said tiredly. 'If only for old time's sake, can't we be friends?'

'Friends!' he husked roughly. 'I don't want to be your damned friend: I want you in my bloody bed.'

'Then you've taken your time in saying so.'

A harsh smile warped his mouth. 'God Almighty! You didn't give me much opportunity.'

'You never even came to see if I was all right.'

'All right? Of course you were all right. Why shouldn't you be all right, I'm not Jack the Ripper, even in my cups . . . ? Oh, I see — ' His eyes flickered. Then he gave a saw-edged laugh. 'That could have proved a rough and ready solution . . . Oh, Beth — ' He pulled her unresisting body to him and cradled her close. 'I must have seemed a right savage. Believe me, my love, I never meant all this to happen. Things just got out of hand. You know me, I'm obstinate, and arrogant, and not one to be pushed around, and when I came bearing the olive branch and you refused to see me . . . Well!' He felt the small movement of surprise she made in his arms and glanced down. 'Yes, I did come. Not the morning after, I admit, I had a king-sized hangover and I was still feeling splendidly sore at the world. But several days later — '

She raised her head, blind-eyed. 'I didn't know,' she whispered.

'Tom said you wouldn't see me — at any price. He threatened to thrash me there and then, told me exactly what he'd do if he ever caught me on this place or bothering you again. With your blessing.' He smiled wryly. 'I couldn't blame you; by then it was seeping through to my consciousness that I'd behaved pretty badly. Which didn't help my ego or my temper . . . I thought, to hell with you; if you didn't want me, there were plenty of other girls who would.'

He pressed her closer to him. She could feel the heavy beating of his heart, the slight trembling of his arm.

'Beth, for what it's worth, it wasn't as bad as they tell it . . . Oh, bad enough, I suppose. But I wasn't the ravening wolf the village would have you believe me these past few months. And the girls were willing.'

'Yes,' said Beth softly, 'I'm sure they were.' There was an odd note in her voice. His eyes flashed to hers suspecting a hidden barb, but found only the glimmer of a teasing smile, then that, too, was gone and the gaze on his was grey velvet. Her arms lifted and locked around him. 'I know exactly how they felt.'

He was home and dry! For a moment

he could hardly believe it. She fitted against him with such sweet familiarity; the stem-slender waist, with the soft swell of her above and below, the lovely, long, firm thighs . . . He wondered if she could feel his immediate violent response to her, and was quite unable to control it. Bending his head in a sudden desperate little movement, he closed her mouth with kisses.

It was several minutes before he was able to say, harshly: 'Tom has a lot to answer for.'

'No! Leave it.' Her tone was sharp. 'If he lied to you it was to protect me, or so he thought. It was my fault: I told him everything. And Tom was never one to stand by and watch me cry.'

'I love you,' Archer said, taking her face in his hands. 'So much. For you, I'll even refrain from smashing Tom's teeth in.' He drew her, still unresisting, across the floor to sit beside him on a heap of straw and kissed her long enough to take her breath away. She surfaced, gasping.

'So that's settled,' he said with satisfaction, lifting his head. 'We'll get married tomorrow. No more nonsense. Six months is a hell of a time to be without you and I can't hold off any longer.'

'Don't be foolish,' she laughed. 'Things can't be organised that quickly.'

'Next week, then.' His fingers were undoing the buttons on her blouse.

'In the middle of harvest? Archer, we'll drive everybody mad.' Her lashes swept down demurely. 'I'm sure we can come to some arrangement for you in the meantime, but — '

'I want you signed, sealed and serviced,' he said. 'I'll see the rector this afternoon, do a little arm-twisting, if necessary. This week, next week — as soon as possible.'

'Archer!' He stilled her protests with his lips.'

'I shall think in a minute that you don't want me,' he murmured. His fingers searched the back of her brassière for the fastening, but encountered only a curve of lace. Returning his attention to the front he found the small hidden clasp under an embroidered rosebud and unhooked it. Released, her breasts rounded into his hands. He pressed her gently down beneath him.

'No, Archer — someone might come.'

'Then they'll have to go away again.'

'Archer — ' She struggled to sit up, tugging her blouse together.

His hands slid from her and he shifted his weight slightly. 'You win,' he said from between clenched teeth. 'Not that way again . . . Ever!'

For a heartbeat their eyes locked, then she leaned slowly back, her arms dropping away to lie defencelessly at her sides. The edge of her blouse slipped, exposing the firm mound of one naked breast.

It was invitation enough.

The hard length of him was upon her, bearing her down, thrusting her into the straw, his hands removing obstacles, cajoling flesh, talking love with practised ease . . .

Distantly, vaguely, as if through a dream, she heard Tom calling to her.

The hands on her stilled.

'Beth? Beth, are you in there?'

'Tom . . . ' Archer's breath went out in a soft little hiss. He held her quiescent under him, saying nothing.

'Beth?'

The bucket! She had forgotten the bucket. It was still standing in the centre of the floor. They felt rather than heard or saw her brother stop to peer through the doorway at the abandoned grain.

One step forward, and he was silhouetted in the opening, a black shape against the brightness of the day beyond.

'Beth?' His figure moved out of the sunshine and he took another pace forward, eyes probing the sudden gloom.

The shadow on the straw split into two parts as Archer pushed himself backwards, away from the girl beneath him.

'Archer Read!' Shock deadened Tom's tone.

Beth sat up slowly. For a second no one spoke, then, as Tom lunged forward, she said, a little breathlessly, her eyes still dazed and slightly unfocused: 'It's all right, Tom . . . ' She clutched her blouse together.

Tom towered over her. 'Get up,' he

commanded harshly. He grabbed her arm and shook her to her feet.

Archer stood to one side, adjusting his belt. A half mocking smile twisted his mouth. 'You do choose your moments, Channing,' he said.

'Tom — ' Beth's voice was unreal in her ears. 'It's quite all right, Tom.'

'That it's not. If he's harmed you — I'll kill him.' He swung a left at Archer's jaw. Archer dodged and Beth caught at Tom's arm before he could swing again.

'Stop it, Tom. It's not what you think . . . '

'I know what I think, and I know Archer Read . . . Button your blouse! . . . He's his leching father all over again.'

'And you should know,' said Archer, 'seeing that you're so very fond of dear Ingham these days.'

'Shut your trap before I shut it for you,' snarled Tom. 'I know what you're after; I'm not as big a fool as you think.'

'Thank God for that!' drawled Archer. He did not move, but his hand clenched and stayed closed.

'Tom, everything's all right, really it is.' Beth gave a nervous little giggle. 'He's come courting again.'

'Has he, by Christ! Is that what you call it, rolling in the straw like a couple of animals? Have you no pride? You know what he's been like these past months, Beth, anything in skirts; and the moment he comes sniffing around again you have to make things easy for him.'

'Jealous, Tom?' asked Archer silkily.

Tom swung his fist with an oath and caught him on the mouth. As Archer reeled back, blood pouring from his lip, Beth sprang to his defence.

Tom swept her aside. 'I'll deal with you later; I should beat you senseless.'

'Excellent,' mumbled Archer through the handkerchief he held to his mouth. 'That should make her see eye-to-eye with you!' He dabbed at his lip. 'It's a pity your strong right arm is allied to such a damned weak head.' He ducked as Tom came at him again. 'Cut it out, Channing. I wasn't raping her. Ask her. She was willing. Look at her — does she look as if I forced her in here?'

If his intention had been to placate Tom, it had the reverse effect. Tom launched himself forward with a cry of fury, arm swinging. But this time Archer was ready for him. He chopped Tom smartly and efficiently on the side of his jaw, jerking his head backwards. Tom stumbled, half recovered himself, then tripped over the bucket that had been standing in the middle of the floor and went down in a clang of metal and spilling grain, hitting his head on the corn-bin.

'Stop it! Stop it!' screamed Beth. 'Stop it, both of you.'

Archer pulled himself clear to allow Tom to struggle painfully to his feet, then walked across to Beth.

Tears were streaming down her cheeks. 'You promised,' she sobbed. 'You promised.'

'It's okay,' he said wearily, 'he's not hurt — much. You can soon patch him up. Treat him for shock.' His lip curled. 'Give him a cup of tea with plenty of sugar and maybe, with luck, he'll sweeten himself to death.'

A shadow winged like a vulture towards him.

Beth shrieked. 'Archer! Look out!'

As Archer whirled, Tom jumped for him with the pitchfork he had tugged from the rack at his side. His face glistened with sweat and his eyes were raging.

The pitchfork whistled forward, driven with all the force of Tom's muscular arms. Forewarned, Archer managed to sidestep and the lethal-seeming thrust caught the outside of his arm instead of piercing his body. The tines ripped through his shirt sleeve and the skin beneath, tearing two parallel grooves in the flesh, wounds that were painful but not dangerous.

Tom poised to strike again.

Beth grabbed her brother's wrists in both hands and held on.

'Okay, okay,' said Archer. 'I'm going. I'm going. Murder doesn't figure in my plans . . . You'd better speak to him, Beth, when he's calmed down a bit; convince him that I don't possess two horns — unless you're keen on having a brawl at our wedding.'

169

'Go home, Archer,' choked Beth.

He turned without another word and walked out through the door.

Beth still clung to her brother's arms. 'Tom, please,' she pleaded. Feeling the tenseness go out from under her fingers, she released her grip.

Tom hurled the pitchfork savagely away from him to hang quivering in the pile of straw. Then he went across to sit on some bales of hay, his head in his hands.

Beth took a small step in his direction before changing her mind and spinning on her heel to run after Archer.

Archer had already reached his car and there was violence in the way he wrenched the door towards him. He slid behind the steering-wheel.

'How's your arm?' husked Beth.

'In great shape,' he replied, with understandable bitterness. 'That maniacal brother of yours should be under lock and key.' He looked up then and stared hard into her eyes. 'One day, my sweet, no matter how you flinch from it, you're going to have to choose between us. One day.' And his car was gone in a shower of gravel.

Slowly Beth retraced her steps to the grain shed. Her brother was sitting as she had left him, defeat in every line of his body. She went forward and rested her hands on his shoulders.

'Don't, Tom,' she whispered. 'Don't.'

'How could you? How could you do it to me?' He raised tormented eyes. 'Anyone but Archer Read. Anyone.'

'Tom, you are my brother and I love you dearly. I always will. All my life you've been a part of me. But I love Archer, too. I've always loved Archer.'

'You must be mad. After all he's done. After all the girls, all the gossip. He's been with some right little tramps. There's talk in the village that he's . . . '

'I don't want to hear what the village says,' said Beth in a cold little voice.

'That's it, then, there's no more to be said. You've made your choice.'

'There is no choice. I love you both. Both! Do you hear? Both of you. I . . . will . . . not . . . choose . . . between . . . you,' she said through gritted teeth.

171

'Tell me something. If he and I were drowning and you could save only one, which would it be?'

Beth said, in exasperation: 'Don't be childish. You can both swim like sea-serpents.'

'Damn you, you can't even answer a straight question with a straight answer, can you? If you marry Archer, can you see him tolerating me near you? Or do you imagine that I'll kowtow to him? No. It will be the end. You won't see me again.'

'Don't be ridiculous. Tom — '

'Damn Archer. And damn you. Damn you both!'

'Have it your own way,' said Beth tiredly, feeling a little sick. 'I'll talk to you when you're in a more agreeable frame of mind.' She turned towards the door.

'And what about Jeff?' he flung after her.

What about Jeff? There had been no particular understanding between them, but she owed him the courtesy of an explanation before he heard the news from elsewhere.

Climbing a stile on her way back from

his farm an hour or so later, she almost fell over Sharon Mumford, who was sitting under a parasol of butterbur in the long grass at the edge of a field just outside the village.

''Lo, Miss Beth,' Sharon said, raising the enormous leaf above her head.

'Hello, Sharon. You're a long way from home. Does your mother know you're here?'

'I'm waiting for Georgie. Mummy's at the Bell. It's her day for the bedrooms.' Her round blue eyes gazed across the field to where the chimneys of the inn could be seen — just — above the tops of the trees. 'Mummy says I must stay within sight of the Bell. And I can see it. There.' A plump finger pointed.

'Yes,' said Beth dubiously, recognising the letter of the law rather than its spirit, 'but — '

'Georgie is supposed to be looking after me,' said Sharon. 'Mummy's very cross with him because she's had to keep me with her this afternoon. He didn't come in for dinner. He's going to get a whopping when he does.' She sighed. 'I wish he'd hurry up, it's not much fun on my own. Georgie tells me stories.'

'Nice ones?'

'Smashing.' Sharon launched into an involved tale of murder, mayhem and gory retribution.

'Sounds like a great T.V. series,' said Beth.

'My brother gave me this.' The child held up a jam-jar full of flowers in which crouched a dejected cuckoo-bee. 'I'm looking after it for him. He's gone back to catch another and, if he does, he's going to let me have this one. It's called Fred.' She shook the jar vigorously, stirring up the inmate.

'Poor little thing,' protested Beth. 'I don't think it likes that. I don't think it likes being in that jar at all. That's a horrible prison and bees prefer to fly free . . . Shall we let it go?'

'I gotta look after it for Georgie,' said Sharon obstinately. 'It's a cuckoo-bee.'

'It will die. Georgie might be ages before he comes home.' Beth resorted to bribery. 'Look, you let the little bee go and I'll show you something my brother used to make for me, when I was a little girl. Would you like that?'

Sharon nodded.

'Undo the lid then.'

'Georgie might be cross.'

'Tell Georgie to see me, if he has any complaints,' said Beth hardily.

She removed the cover from the jar and watched the cuckoo-bee crawl away. It was some minutes before it recovered sufficiently to fly.

'I don't think Mummy should whop Georgie because he missed his dinner, do you?' whispered Sharon.

'I doubt if your mother's really angry about the meal; I expect she's cross because she's not sure where your brother is, and that worries her.'

'What was it your brother used to make for you?'

'Poppy dolls. Watch.' Beth picked a poppy and deftly folded the petals downwards to form a skirt, which she bound around at the waist with a blade of grass. A length of stalk formed arms when slipped between the sections of the bodice.

'It's only got one leg,' objected Sharon.

'It's meant to be a ballerina on her points . . . ' Beth laughed. 'But if you're fussy — ' She twisted a second stem and tucked it somewhat insecurely beside the first.

'That's nice,' said Sharon. 'Can we make another?'

Side by side in the fragrant grass, Beth and the small child sat, absorbed, the sun hot on their heads, the scent of stray late honeysuckles in their nostrils. Away to their left a tractor hummed across a field of stubble, carving the earth into straight brown furrows.

When Beth eventually lifted her eyes it was to see Mrs Mumford hurrying along the road towards them, still clad in her apron. And Sharon was borne swiftly back to the Bell.

Unwilling to return home herself to her mother's questions and her brother's grievances, Beth spent the rest of the afternoon and the early evening with an old schoolfriend and, when she retraced her steps past the place where she had been sitting with Sharon earlier that day, dusk was already beginning to fall. A discarded poppy doll lay forgotten at the edge of the roadside, limp and dying, all its brave scarlet faded away. Beth picked it up.

The first poppy doll she had ever seen had been made for her by Tom. As he had made and done so many other things for her. She tossed the wilted petals into the grass, remembering. When she had been a small child, it had been Tom who had taken her to school and brought her home again and later helped her with her homework; one year older than she was, he had always been one jump ahead. He had fought her battles, vetted her friends, teased her, laughed with her, loved her. Taught her, sometimes, more than he should. Her eyes blanked. It was unthinkable that she could remain on bad terms with her brother.

She found him sitting in his room by the window, his body slumped forward across a table, his head resting on his folded arms. Beyond the open curtains the first star hovered like a ghost moth above the apple-tree.

Tom sat up with a sharp little defensive movement as Beth shut the door behind her. Crossing the floor to him on swift feet, she put her arms about his neck and her cheek against his hair.

'Tom, I'm sorry. Don't let's quarrel. Please. I can't bear it,' she whispered.

His arms closed about her wordlessly.

She was still standing firmly clasped, with his face pressed to her breast, when Mrs Mumford walked out of the twilight and headed for the house.

A moment later T.J. called up the stairs. 'Tom! Beth! Come down here. Georgie Mumford is missing.'

9

The child was still missing the following day. Search-parties had been organised and police with dogs were combing the area. And every farm for miles around now released its workforce to check barns and outlying buildings, anywhere where a child might be tempted to play and come to grief. In spite of the pressures of harvest, the village of Otley Ash turned out in strength, but to no avail. Georgie Mumford remained missing.

Somebody reported having seen children playing by the gravel-pit lakes the day before, one boy with hair the colour of the eye-catching Mumford beacon. Was it Georgie? No one seemed to know. Yet all recognised that a child in difficulties in forty feet of icy water stood little chance. So it was with a sense of fatality that people watched police frogmen preparing for an arduous exploration of the depths.

Doggedly, the small bands of searchers

continued their own hunt across the countryside, beating through the belts of hawthorn and bramble, scouring the hazel thickets, hoping against hope that they would find the boy, injured perhaps, in some derelict barn or overgrown ditch, or trapped unseen on some waste place among the tall, pungent wormwood.

But the day was fading towards evening before Georgie Mumford was found.

He was discovered lying, face downwards, in a shallow pool of rusty water at the bottom of an abandoned water-tank in Hanged Man's Wood, several miles from the village of Otley Ash. It was presumed that he had been playing there, climbed and fallen. There was a length of old rope knotted to the girder-work below the tank, and a few short planks and pieces of timber tied to the catwalk that ran around the base of the tank proper, as if he had been constructing some kind of camping-place or eyrie among the tree-tops.

Stunned, the village drifted back about its business.

'I don't understand it,' Beth said to

Tom, the next day. 'Why should Georgie Mumford have been in Hanged Man's Wood?'

'Why should any youngster do any of the stupid things he does?' returned Tom. 'It's enough that he does them. All the time. Can't you remember being ten years old? You know what we were like. Why, Archer, and you and I used to — '

'I know — ' cut in Beth primly. 'We were very naughty.'

He laughed. 'I'd put it stronger than that — sometimes.'

'Yes. But we were together. Why should Georgie go to a place like that all alone? Where were his friends?'

Tom shrugged and grounded the heavy metal shaft he had been holding. They were outside the forge, at noon, unloading various pieces of iron and steel from the Land-Rover.

'What's the jungle for?' He pushed aside an armful of flowers to reach some ploughshares.

'I promised Lucy I'd take them to the church. Careful! Don't knock all the heads off,' protested Beth, as Tom decapitated a red rose. 'Those are the long-lasting ones for the altar.'

'That one didn't last long.'

'No. I'd better take them safely inside . . . You can manage here, can't you?'

He nodded, watching her fill her arms with flowers.

She eyed him across the bunch of blooms. 'I don't think Georgie went to the wood alone. And I certainly don't believe he would have climbed that water-tank by his own choice.'

'What are you driving at?'

'Georgie had no head for heights. He suffered from vertigo. He wouldn't even go up the church spire with his friends, nor climb to the top of Reads' windmill. So why would he suddenly decide to scramble up some gruesome girdering and fall inside a water-tank?'

'For a dare, perhaps?'

'Maybe. I've thought about that, too. But it still doesn't seem likely to me. I spoke to him in the churchyard and he was scared rigid of heights. If he had been dared to do it, he'd have wriggled out of it some way, I'm sure. Besides, no one has said anything.'

'They wouldn't, would they?'

'No, perhaps not.' She glanced at him. 'Would *you* go up that spider-thin ladder on the water-tank in Hanged Man's Wood?'

'Of course not. But then you know that I — ' He broke off, staring at her. 'I see what you mean. It's not just a case of wouldn't climb it, but couldn't climb it, isn't it? . . . But Mrs Mumford must have told the police all this.'

'If she knew. Georgie kept the fact pretty dark, I imagine. He was terribly ashamed of himself.'

'Poor little blighter, I know how he felt.' Tom's voice was bitter. 'But T.J. hardly encouraged me in that particular little weakness.'

'Then how did the child get there?' demanded Beth.

They stared at each other for a long moment in silence.

'Exactly!' said Beth, turning on her heel.

After she had deposited her flowers in the church porch beside an enormous pile of cardboard boxes, Beth walked pensively back through the churchyard. On an impulse, she swung off the main path and approached the gravestone where she had been sitting with Georgie earlier in the week. Her hand on the warm stone, she looked upwards at the spire's slender pointing finger. In her ears she could hear the rough little voice, see the pebbles falling among the flowerheads, remember the strained attempt at laughter.

Sighing, she moved on, wandering to and fro among the gravestones, her feet silent on the turf, her skirt brushing the seeding grasses. A vase had fallen from one of the marble plinths. She straightened it; picked a paper bag from another. Then, beside one of the older, tumbled headstones, she saw it. A jam-jar, lidded and full of withered flowers. It was lying on its side. Slowly Beth stooped and picked it up, holding the glass to catch the light. There was something else in the bottom with the debris. A dead cuckoo-bee.

But what did that prove? She frowned. Only that Georgie had been there and, then, only to her. Yet —

'Bethany!'

Beth gave a start and placed the jam-jar on the nearest gravestone. 'Mr Waterhouse — ' Fixing a smile on her lips she stepped forward to meet the rector.

'Ah, Bethany . . . I wanted a word — '

'I can't stay,' warned Beth. The rector's word was apt to be elastic. 'Tom is waiting for me by the forge.'

But the Reverend Waterhouse was already launched. 'I had to see you. I've had a visit from Archer — ' Dimly Beth was aware of the gist of his conversation and she nodded sagely in most of the right places, but her mind was far away, concerned with a small red-haired boy and a dead bee.

'That's agreeable to you, then?' Mr Waterhouse was saying, as Beth nodded. 'Three weeks . . . earliest . . . must come and see . . . both of you . . . talk . . . ' Beth went on nodding like a demented mandarin. The rector, coming to the end of his considerable monologue, looked at her oddly. He had the uncomfortable feeling that Bethany Channing had digested nothing he had said.

'Here's Tom, now,' she murmured, with obvious relief.

Her brother must have heard the tail-end of the discourse because he greeted the rector and said: 'I see you already know about Beth and her intended. Archer didn't waste much time.' He gave the rector a brittle smile. 'Still, there's many a slip betwixt cup and lip — as my old granny used to say.'

'What old granny? Tom!' Beth eyed him with misgiving as he turned to her, afraid that he was about to make some kind of scene, but he fixed her with a glittering look. For the present, at least, he was content to go along with her wishes.

Taking Beth by the arm, he said: 'Come on, old girl, we haven't got all afternoon.' He lifted a thick dark brow at the rector. 'I see you're busy. What is it? Moving day?'

'These are the goods from the church, all the decorations and craftwork. They have to be returned to those who so kindly loaned them for the concert.' There was a shadow on the rector's face.

186

'I'm cancelling the bazaar and the amusement stalls. I don't see how, after this appalling tragedy, we can have a day of jollity. Not so soon. Terrible business, terrible . . . I thought that later, perhaps, we might have a small sale of work to provide funds for some kind of memorial for the child. I need time to discuss it with people . . . ' His voice trailed away as he stared forlornly at the cardboard cartons piled at his side. 'I must go to Mrs Mumford again — Poor woman, poor woman.'

'Would you like help with these?' asked Beth gently.

He brightened. 'I would be most grateful. If you could deliver one or two of the bulkier items — ?'

'Of course.' Beth went over to the pile of boxes. 'I see they have names marked on the outside. We can take Esther's along to her.' She stooped to pick up a medium-sized carton with *Deauville* scrawled across it. 'Hell, this is heavy. What's in it? Rocks?'

'They're Miss Deauville's plaques,' said the rector, his tone apologetic. 'I'm afraid they are indeed very weighty. Maybe your brother — '

Tom swung the box up in his arms without a word.

'There are three other containers for Miss Deauville,' went on the rector, sorting through the arrangement at his side, 'and these two for Browning, if you could drop them off as you go past — ?'

'No problem,' replied Beth. She carried the goods to the gate and stowed them in the back of the Land-Rover. Then said to her brother: 'I'll leave you at the farm and cart these up to Esther's myself, if you like. I know you're behindhand again at the oast after the search for Georgie.'

'Who cares,' said Tom, slamming into the driving-seat.

Beth glanced at him in surprise. As he turned towards her she caught the faint smell of whisky on his breath.

'Have you been in the Bell?'

'For a quick one,' he laughed.

For a couple of quick ones, thought Beth. And doubles, from the sound of it.

'I think you'd better let me have the wheel.'

'My dear Beth, *you* I'd let have anything.'

'Stop messing about,' she scowled, 'and move over. And stop grinning like a jackass, it's hardly the time or place for it.' She elbowed him aside. 'I've been thinking about Georgie Mumford.'

'And so have I.' His face sobered. 'So have I.'

Quickly, as they went along, Beth explained about the dead bee and her meeting with Sharon the day the boy disappeared.

'Sharon said George had gone to find another cuckoo-bee. Evidently he found one.' She glanced at her brother. 'Don't you think it's strange that he didn't take it back to her?'

Tom raised a shoulder. 'Probably something else caught his attention and he left his jar in the churchyard, meaning to return for it.'

'I suppose so.'

Her brother shot her a look. 'You're still not satisfied are you? You still don't believe he climbed that tower by himself.'

'Do you?'

He shrugged helplessly.

'And if he didn't,' said Beth, 'then it means that someone must have taken him up there. Deliberately.'

'Beth! You can't go around accusing someone of murder.'

'I'm not.'

'That's what it amounts to, though. If the child didn't go there of his own free will, and someone took him there, to drown — ' Tom drew in his breath slightly. A muscle twitched at the corner of his eye. 'It doesn't make sense. Why would anyone want to do away with Georgie Mumford?'

'There's a great deal, at the moment, that doesn't make sense. Why should Violet Pettifer have eaten a basketful of Death Caps?'

'It was an accident — it must have been.'

'But it was Georgie who said that Violet had received those toadstools as a gift. He told us so. Maybe someone wished to keep him quiet.'

'Beth!' Tom was very white. 'No one would kill him for that. Why should they?

There would be no point. He must have told lots of people the same thing . . . You and I, and Lucy, for a start. And his mother, I imagine, and probably dozens of others. He liked to feel important. If what you are implying was the case, then at least half the village would have to be silenced.'

'Yes, of course.' She looked relieved.

'The police will go into things if there's anything to go into.'

'Yes, I suppose so.'

'Two people dead — by accident — and you would have Otley Ash a hotbed of crime.'

'Three people.'

Tom stared at her.

Beth said: 'You seem to have forgotten the man found dead in the ditch.'

'That had nothing to do with the village. That was an unlucky coincidence. He just happened to die on our doorstep.'

'Thoughtless of him,' said Beth, bringing the Land-Rover to rest beside Esther's terrace. She jumped out and walked round to the rear of the vehicle to begin unloading the boxes. As she did so,

Reuben Colley charged past, almost knocking her down. His dark eyes looked murderous and there were two thin wheals across his left cheekbone, as if he had received a couple of cuts from a switch. He made no attempt to apologise for bumping into her, nor did he speak to Tom, who had also alighted from the Land-Rover, but continued his angry stride towards the gate.

'What's the matter with him?' gasped Beth.

'Your guess is as good as mine,' returned Tom, 'but I shouldn't fancy crossing him at the moment. He looks as if he'd like to stick a knife into someone.' He turned to greet Esther, who had just come from the cellar across to them. They could not help but notice she was carrying a thin piece of the cane she used for staking her more delicate flowers. She, too, looked angry, her golden eyes snapping.

Beth explained why they were there, and gestured at the boxes. Esther barely thanked them. Her gaze was following the retreating man along the drive.

'What was Reuben doing here?' asked Tom.

'That, young Tom, is none of your business. As what Reuben is sticking his finger into is none of his.' She waved towards the terrace. 'Stand those boxes on the table there, for now.' Then she went down to the cellar entrance again, slammed the door she had left open and locked it.

Tom said: 'I should watch your step with him, Esther. He's not a man to forgive a grudge.'

Esther savaged him with a glance. 'You're not so lily-pure, Tom Channing. Concentrate on riding your own cock-horse.'

'Tom's right,' ventured Beth. 'Reuben looked wild.'

'Reuben Colley will risk anything for money, even his neck,' said Esther cryptically, dropping the cellar key into her pocket. They watched her without speaking. 'And now, I'm busy, so good day to you.'

'What on earth do you think she's got down in that cellar?' whispered Beth to her brother, as they climbed back into the Land-Rover.

'Rats, probably,' said Tom shortly. He looked tired, with shadows under his eyes, and the brief lift the whisky had given him had worn off. Neither of them had had any sleep the night of Georgie's disappearance, and very little on the one following, and neither of them was going to have an easy day. T.J. was already in the yard screaming for blood when they drove in and parked alongside the grain-shed.

'See you, Tom,' murmured Beth cravenly, sliding from her seat and scurrying across to the house.

Where Reuben had got to she had no idea, they had not passed him on the road, nor — as was apparent from her father's incipient apoplexy — had he reached the oast. Whether he did so in the next hour or so, she was too busy to find out. Tom she did not see again that day. It was past midnight before he came in, and Beth was already in her room, preparing for bed, when she saw him cross the yard and pass under the apple-tree outside the window. He paused there for a few moments, staring up at the sky, as if praying for a fine day on the morrow. Again she thought how tired he looked, his face scoured colourless by moonlight. Haggard. As if some flame inside him had been brutally quenched. Then he swung and came on towards her.

With a jolt, Beth realised that her brother was not quite steady on his feet. Not normally a hard drinker, he had obviously taken a little too much on board that evening. A worried frown creased her forehead. She heard him stumble upstairs and walk slowly to the bathroom, and the swish of running water as he turned on the taps. Then silence. Somewhere, beyond the distant woods, a dog barked. Beth let out her breath gently, in relief; T.J. was fortunately asleep.

The moonlight wheeled across the floor, bright as day, carrying the shadows of the trees and the nodding flowerheads which twined around her window. The scent of mint geranium wafted to her from the border below.

Faintly, at last, she heard Tom's

footsteps padding along the corridor to his room. They hesitated outside. Moved on. Stopped. Seconds later her door opened and he stood framed in the entrance, his hands lifting to press against the jamb on either side of him.

'Tom!' She gave a low, involuntary cry. His face was like death, his grey eyes bloodshot and wearing the strange blind stare of one condemned to everlasting darkness. 'Tom — ' She went suddenly still.

He came into the room and closed the door behind him . . .

* * *

Esther, too, at Elderwood, had been watching the circling shadows of the moonlight; the traceries of the tall ash-trees patterning the lawn, the barred slashes of the orchard fence-stakes thrown into stark relief along the driveway, the border of denser gloom beside the hawthorn hedges. Dew silvered the grass.

Standing on the terrace, she strained her eyes to see beyond the darkness of the boundary wood. Twice she had heard a dog bark and twice that number of times had come downstairs from her bed to unlatch the door. But Pym had failed to materialise. She bit her lip. Half-blind and stiff of limb, the old dog was not given to wandering, yet he had been missing since early evening and all her frantic calling had not brought him waddling back to her. Worried, she was certain now that he must have been trapped somewhere in the woods, but there was little she could do until the morning.

For one brief moment, as she stared towards the trees, she thought she saw a movement, a trembling of the shadows, a flash of white like moonlight fingering a face, a quiver so slight and so quickly gone that she imagined she must have been mistaken. All was still. Quiet. If anyone had been around the geese would have given her ample warning. Her eyes darted to their huddled shapes, moonpale under the magnolia tree. Nothing there to disturb her. And yet —

Shivering, unaccountably uneasy, Esther

turned and made her way back to bed.

When she woke again it was morning, very early, with the sun not yet risen. A quick pot of tea later, and she was pulling on her boots, scrambling into her coat and letting herself out into the polished dawn. Spiders' webs, heavy with moisture, were spun over every bush and looped in beaded strands from flowerhead to flowerhead. The tall grass at the edge of the lawn was grey with their embroideries. Everywhere was quiet. Too quiet. Her gaze flew to the geese, still hunched palely under their magnolia-tree.

In the clear morning light their tranquillity took on a more sinister aspect. It hardly needed a closer inspection to tell her that they would never move again. There was not a mark on them, but they were stiff and cold, huddled together in the frozen immobility of death. Esther's hands trembled against the cloth of her coat. For a heartbeat she found herself snatched back in horror to another time, another such confrontation, when, as a small child, she had stood beside her mother, with their dead hens littering the ground.

She shook herself. This was now. Whoever had done this had done it with neatly calculated malice. Had done it, too, very cleverly. And how? Poison? It seemed the most likely explanation and the only one she could think of which would have allowed the killer access to the birds without her knowledge. Yesterday, sometime, when the place had been full of comings and goings, when fruit-pickers had been in the orchard and packers and buyers and trucks milling around the drive. When anybody could have mingled in the company, unremarked and unchallenged. Half the village seemed to have been there at one point or another and anyone could have administered a lethal dose of a slow-acting poison. Anyone. Esther felt sick. But what kind of person would settle a grudge in such a fashion? She knew she had enemies; she was too outspoken and too sharp of tongue to have reached her present span of years without upsetting a few of the local folk. She could think of at least half a score who might have cause to bear her ill-will. But none to hit back at her in such a manner.

Far away, from the direction of the wood, a dog howled.

With a sudden hollowness in the pit of her stomach, she remembered Pym. If he had been harmed . . .

Walking away from the dead geese, she paused only to collect a stout stick with which to beat aside the blackberry tentacles before heading for the wood.

The night's dew lay glittering on the ferns and dripped from the trees above her. There was the bitter-sweetness of wet, rotting leaves and sodden bracken hanging in the air; a lush damp greenness on every side, with here and there a touch of brilliant colour where the brambles were turning. Her feet made no sound on the thick mould as she hurried along. Among the mossy roots shone jewel-like toadstools, the scarlet Fly Agaric, poison-ous and beloved of illustrators of fairy tales, and some purplish-tinged Deceiv-ers. And fat green nuts crowded thick upon the hazel branches. The ground grew rougher and more tangled with undergrowth the further she penetrated into the wood, but there was a path, of sorts, and the occasional despairing howl of the dog kept her struggling onwards.

She stopped to listen. The keening was closer now, persistent, a panic note that tuned into the painful throbbing of her heart.

It came to her gradually that she was not alone. Little snaps of sound and soft rustlings which she had not immediately noticed were now breaking in upon her consciousness. The crackle of dead twigs when her feet were still, a whisper of falling soil behind her, the faint scratch of something against a tree-trunk. Almost, she was persuaded she could hear alien footsteps.

Halting once more to catch her breath, she peered warily around her. Everywhere was thick and tangled, rich and green with late summer, the leaves not yet beginning to fall. Somebody could be hiding in any one of a dozen places. Or in none. Now there was no sound except the faint sighing of the breeze in the tree-tops.

Breathing heavily, she grasped her stick and pressed her way forward. It would take more than a stealthy follower to frighten Esther Deauville, she thought, grim-lipped.

Besides, if anyone had wished to attack her, there had been abundant opportunity anywhere along the blackberry-straggled path. The fact that she was still safe must have meant that no mischief was intended. Her fancies were getting the better of her.

The trees were thinner here, the foliage less dense, sunmotes spilling through the leaves; she was coming to the edge of the wood where the ground fell away along a chalky ridge. There was no way down to the dell, forty feet beneath her, at least, not from this point. The sides ran sheer to the grassy area below. She could see piles of white rock among the golden ragwort where chalk had fallen from the cliff edge above, and, elsewhere, bushes of elder and dogwood and trails of honeysuckle, with the fiery flames of gorse licking upwards on the slopes on the far side.

None of that, however, held her

attention. To one side of a heap of stone just below her lay a splintered tree-trunk and, by that, a dog's body, stretched. For one terrible leap of the heart she thought he must have been dead, then his head twitched and she heard the low whine.

'Pym!'

At her call he bounded up and began to rush round in tight circles, barking and straining to look up at her. She could not see properly how he was held, his limbs appeared to be free, but somehow he was caught, anchored to the tree-trunk beside him. It looked for all the world as if he had a piece of rope or twine twisted around his neck and slowly strangling him. She peered into the depths, leaning outwards at an angle to see how she might make her way in safety to his trap.

Then the day split violently apart.

She felt a sudden tremendous heave against her shoulders and found herself launched forward, spinning into space, plunging helplessly down towards the rocks below.

10

The sun was well up, shining full on the chalk-face where Esther hung motionless, like a dead spider from a broken web. One of her flailing arms had caught, crooked over, between the cliff and a small bush growing from a fissure in the stone, and her clutching fingers had done the rest, snapping desperately closed on their fragile support.

For a short while she had thought that she was indeed dead, the shock of her swoop into space and the sickening jerk which broke her fall rendering her almost unconscious. But gradually she realised that she was still breathing, suspended painfully between heaven and earth with only one arm and one frail piece of vegetation separating her from a probable fractured skull below. Just how frail, she found out as soon as she attempted to raise her other arm to ease the strain upon its fellow. The bush bent out at an alarming angle from its anchorage at her slightest move. Her free arm was almost useless. It did not appear to be broken, but somehow, in her fall, she must have banged it cruelly against the cliff. Already badly bruised by the goose's beak, it now reacted to its rough treatment with total numbness; even her fingers refused to close.

By dint of careful manoeuvring she managed to wedge her shoulder and upper arm between the base of the bush and the chalk-face and to grope for a toe-hold with her feet in the uneven surface of the rock. But as she settled with a sigh of relief the roots of the bush pulled a little freer and she felt herself sag downwards, her feet scrabbling wildly for another hold. Small rivulets of crumbled stone chased down the cliff in whispering runnels to the ground.

Dizzily she looked about her. The whiteness of the chalk splintered against her eyes. She dared not lean outwards to glance down, dared hardly breathe. Any sudden movement caused her handhold to become more insecure. Esther felt the sweat start on her body.

Was anyone at the top of the cliff? She could hear nothing, see nothing. Even Pym was now silent below. Whoever had pushed her to disaster did not appear to have stayed to complete the job. But then, she thought bitterly, it was hardly necessary. A short half hour and either her strength or her anchorage would give way and her body would be lying, smashed, among the rocks in the dell. An accident.

Despair caught at her throat. She tried to clamp her uninjured arm more firmly around the bush and another whisper of chalk debris went sliding past her into the depths.

As the gentle rattle died away another sound reached her, from above. And, for an instant, she froze. A footstep? A slight rustle of cloth? The would-be murderer returned? Too terrified to call out, she licked bone-dry lips.

'Esther?'

The voice came to her, soft and slight through the sunshine, almost as if she were dreaming. Then again, more insistent.

'Esther!'

'Beth Channing,' croaked Esther. 'Thank God.'

Beth's face peered down at her.

'Esther! Esther, what are you *doing*?'

'Not admiring the view, that's for sure,' snapped Esther. 'For heaven's sake! Don't just stand there. Pull me up.'

'I can't. I can't reach you.'

'Oh, lord,' groaned Esther, 'of all the tom-fool answers, Beth Channing . . . Do something! Give me your hand.'

'I can't reach you. I haven't arms like a gorilla.'

'A gorilla'd be a damned sight more use at the moment — '

'Keep calm, Esther. I'll have to find help.'

'No!' Esther's voice rang out in desperation. 'No. There's no time. This bush is going, I can feel it. I've wedged a foot in a crack here to take some of my weight, but that's crumbling too.' Besides, her assailant might return.

'Two minutes,' said Beth firmly. 'I've the Land-Rover parked on the track just beyond the bushes. Hang on.'

'What else?' breathed Esther bitterly.

But Beth was back within the promised time, gasping, as if she had been running hard.

'Esther?' She peered downwards. 'I've a rope. It's secured this end.' A length of nylon cord snaked down towards Esther. 'There. Can you climb it?'

'No,' said Esther.

Beth's face appeared above her again.

'Well, catch hold of it, then; it'll be safer than hanging on to that bush. And I'll try to haul you up.'

'I can't,' said Esther. 'My left arm is almost useless, there's no strength in it, and I can't let go with the other or I shall fall.'

There was silence for a moment.

'All right,' said Beth. 'I'll come down and put the rope around you and then I'll pull you up . . . If I can,' she added hopefully.

Esther closed her eyes. Hysterical laughter was bubbling against her lips. Briefly she wondered if her attacker was watching and, if so, what he or she would do. Her eyes flicked open.

'No!' she shouted. 'Stay where you are, Beth. Loop the rope and send it back down. Try to guide it over my shoulders and I'll wriggle it into place the best I can with my bruised arm.'

Within seconds the noose was slipping over her head. Beth fumbled the rope sideways.

'Down a bit. Round my waist,' said Esther tartly. 'It's not a necktie party.'

'If you could just help yourself a little more,' gasped Beth. 'It's very awkward . . . There. That looks about right.' She nodded with satisfaction at her handi-work. 'Does it feel comfortable?'

'I'm not going to wear it permanently,' retorted Esther, with a certain sourness. 'It'll do.'

'At least you can't tumble. I'll soon have you safely out of this.'

'Get on with it,' snarled Esther, bracing her feet against the chalk-face and taking a firm hold on the rope with her undamaged hand. She watched Beth disappear from view.

A second later the girl's voice floated down.

'I've had a better idea. I'm going to try to bring the Land-Rover round, if I can. To drag you up. I don't think I can manage your weight by myself. Don't worry. You're quite secure.'

Secure! thought Esther bitterly. Like a blessed bobbin on a string! It was to be hoped that no one was waiting above with a knife poised to sever her life-line. She shuddered, cracking her ears for the sound of the Land-Rover grinding in for the rescue.

It seemed a very long time coming.

'Thank you,' said Esther, when she was at last standing square, giddy and breathless, but safe, beside Beth at the top of the cliff. 'That's one I owe you, Beth Channing.' Her bumps and bruises ached but, on examination, she appeared to be in one unbroken piece.

Beth smiled. 'That'll teach you not to fall off cliffs,' she said, neatly coiling the rope and returning it to the rear of the vehicle. 'It was very silly to go so near the edge.'

'When I want your advice,' snapped Esther, 'I'll ask for it. Besides, I didn't

210

fall. I was pushed.'

Beth grinned at her in disbelief, her brows raised. 'Oh, yes?'

'Take that moronic expression off your face, girl,' said Esther crossly. 'I'm telling you the simple truth. Someone came behind me and shoved me over the edge. Deliberately.'

'Who would push you off a cliff?'

'I don't know, do I? I didn't see anyone. But someone who wants to be rid of me, I should think.'

'Then they'd have stayed to make sure you were finished, wouldn't they?'

'Well, you came along and frightened them off, I suppose. I thought I heard a car start up soon after I fell. Did you see anyone, Beth?'

The girl shook her head. 'I'd parked the Land-Rover on the back track and I was walking over there — ' She nodded to the slopes on the far side of the dell. 'It's peaceful there; a good place to go if you want to be alone.' The dark lashes swept down over the grey eyes that were so like Tom's. 'I spotted your bright coat against the white cliff-face and came round to investigate. Lucky I did.'

'Very lucky for me,' said Esther, her tone dry. 'I'd have been a goner in another ten minutes.' She rubbed her painful arm ruefully. 'I'm getting too old for this kind of thing.'

Beth glanced at her curiously. 'Why were you here in the first place?'

'I came after Pym. He was down there, trapped in the dell.'

'He's not there now,' said Beth, eyeing the quiet, sunny area below them.

'No. Perhaps he gnawed free.' Esther winced as she stepped away from the edge.

'Come along, I'll drive you home,' said Beth. She helped the older woman round to the passenger-seat of the Land-Rover. 'We'd better ask the doctor to take a look at you.'

'Benson's coming this afternoon, anyhow.'

'Good. Lie back and relax,' Beth said, leaning forward to fold a rug behind her companion's head. The sun was bright on her face and, for the first time that morning, Esther studied the features of her rescuer keenly. She thought the girl looked drawn and desperately tired. Almost hag-ridden. With faint shadows blueing the fine skin under her eyes. And her lips had that kind of swollen, bee-stung look that could come as the result of a blow — or from too many kisses. Someone, it seemed, had been using her hard.

Aware of Esther's scrutiny, Beth turned her face away sharply and hurried to clamber into the driving-seat. But not before Esther had caught a glimpse of the bruising on her neck; round dark marks like purple pansies against the delicate flesh.

Beth, feigning not to notice the older woman's open stare, slammed the vehicle into gear and moved away, bumping over the rough terrain and flattening the already battered-down brambles, to pull out on to the track that flung its arms across the top of the downland. The track provided a rear access route for many of the higher farms. Turning to the right, she headed in the direction of Elderwood.

'I'll detail some of the boys to look for Pym,' she said.

Esther shook her head. 'There's no need. If he's free, then he'll find his way home.'

'And I'll contact Jim Tate for you,' Beth added, as the Land-Rover swung round the back drive to deposit Esther at her door.

'Jim Tate?' Esther sounded bewildered. 'Why?'

'So that you may tell him about your accident,' said Beth. 'If you really believe that you were pushed — '

'Of course I was pushed. I'm not suffering from delusions, if that's what you think,' returned Esther. 'Although doubtless that's what everyone will say. 'Just like her mother',' mimicked Esther. She looked at Beth from under scowling brows. 'You weren't too keen on believing me, so why should anybody else? So, no police. And no spreading this tale abroad. There are certain people who would be only too pleased to have me trundled away in a little padded van.'

'Having reached the ripe old age of

seventy with no symptoms of mental disorder, I should think you're quite safe,' said Beth dryly. 'But, as you wish. I was concerned with your welfare. If what you say is true, then someone tried to kill you. And, whether you like it or not, I'm going to tell Jim Tate.'

Esther grabbed her arm. 'You will not. You'll keep your nose out of my affairs. I don't want any more stupid questions or any more big feet trampling my property.' She glared. 'I can look after myself. I have my father's old shotgun and I know how to use it. I'm not your average helpless old woman, not by a long chalk.'

'I know that,' said Beth. 'You're as stubborn as a mule and with about as much sense. Suppose whoever tried to tip you over that cliff tries something else equally nasty? What then?'

'Then I'll be ready for it.'

Beth sighed in exasperation. 'Esther — ' She got no further. Her eyes had come to rest on the geese, hunched stiffly in their awkward attitudes under the magnolia-tree. 'My God — ' she whispered. Her eyes flew back to Esther. 'What in heaven's name has been happening?'

Esther shrugged. 'Poisoned, I think. It seems someone bears me a grudge.'

'A grudge? Is that what you call it? This is sick. Whoever killed these birds must be mentally deranged. It's a madman we're dealing with.'

'Or madwoman.' Esther turned. 'Leave it, Beth. It's best forgotten. It'd be said they'd eaten deadly nightshade.' Her voice was bitter. 'If you mention anything, anything at all, about what has happened today, I shall deny it. I shall say my fall was an accident and that you are making a mountain out of a molehill . . . Perhaps I did trip, after all. Can you prove that I didn't? It's an explanation which would save a lot of bother.'

'And was this an accident?'

Esther looked gravely down at the dead birds. 'No. But it was one of the things my mother was accused of doing. Killing poultry. Her own and other people's.' Her eyes were cloudy and far away. 'And a village never forgets. It has a kind of collective memory. I've endured the whispers and garbled tales all my life. I have only to deviate one hair's-breadth from the suffocating norm and there's some bright spark ready to point a finger — 'Oh, you know what her mother was like . . . '.' She gave a small laugh. 'My mother suffered from a persecution complex. She believed everyone was out to get her, even out to kill her. She accused people of terrible things; attempts on her life, attempts to harm her livestock. In the end it was proved she had been doing the things herself . . . '

'I'm sorry,' said Beth inadequately. She frowned slightly. 'About the geese — There is another possibility. If Pym were required as a decoy, then the death of the geese would have simplified the matter of his removal.'

'Melodramatic. But I had thought of that,' replied Esther. She staggered and Beth ran to catch her shoulders.

'Esther, come inside. Come and rest. You've had a shock and you're hurt, come and lie down,' pleaded Beth. 'I'll make you a cup of tea; tuck you up . . . ' Wheedling, pleading, she assisted the old woman inside the house and persuaded her to lie on the sofa. Go upstairs she would not.

'Stop fussing,' said Esther. 'I'm feeling fine. A little tired, that's all. I was up half the night.' She shot the girl a sly glance. 'Like you, from the looks of it.'

Beth turned away to brew a pot of tea and then began to tidy up.

'Beth Channing, go home do,' said Esther in exasperation.

'I don't like to leave you alone.'

'I've been alone for thirty years of my life, a little more isn't going to harm me.'

'That wasn't what I meant and you know it.'

'Send Reuben up here,' said Esther suddenly. 'He can stay here, be my watch-dog. There's an old caravan in the orchard he can have.' She scowled darkly. 'Seeing that most of this is probably his fault, it's only right he should suffer a little of the discomfort.'

'Reuben's fault?' Beth stared at her. 'You mean, Reuben killed the geese? Reuben pushed you over the cliff?'

'Of course Reuben didn't push me over the cliff. Why should he? Reuben has his own fish to fry.' She laughed at Beth's worried face. 'Reuben is family and, whatever the Colleys may or may not be, they stick by their own. No, he'd never hurt me . . . '

Beth studied her thoughtfully for a moment. 'What's he been up to?'

'Oh, his usual activities, nine-tenths outside the law . . . Our Reuben has sticky fingers.' Esther drew her brows together in a grim line. 'And of all the hare-brained schemes I'd ever heard, his latest was just about the wildest. Like lifting a bone from a tiger's paw. I tried to dissuade him, but I'm beginning to suspect he might have decided to go ahead with a bit of arm-twisting, instead.' She stood her empty teacup on the table beside her. 'Anyhow, send him up to me quickly, girl. I'll soon straighten him out.'

'I don't doubt it.' Beth wheeled and went into the hall, where she paused to hang Esther's coat on its familiar hook. As she did so, there was a slight clunk of something hard against the hall-stand. Thinking that Esther must have left her key-ring in the pocket, Beth slid in her hand and removed the hidden object. Not a bunch of keys as she had been expecting, but a single large one which she recognised as being the key Esther had used on the cellar door.

For a few seconds Beth stared at it. Then, still gripping it in her hand, she went outside and down the steps to the cellar. Whatever Esther was keeping locked in there was obviously not for prying eyes. In spite of what the old woman had said, had Reuben already prevailed upon her to store some ill-gotten gains?

There was one way to find out.

Beth fitted the key into the lock and pushed open the door when the catch clicked back.

It was dark in the cellar, cobweb-cauled across the beamed ceiling and smelling of mould. Yes, quite definitely smelling of mould — the damp, chrysanthemum-like smell of rotting leaves and moist earth. She took a step forward. The one small window was warped and covered in grime, allowing little light to spill between its fossilised frames. But what amount there was scored the raised ground beside her feet.

Beth stared down, her eyes widening. Whatever she had expected, it certainly was not this.

Even as she stooped forward, hand outstretched, the cellar darkened as the door slammed closed behind her. She heard the scrape of a key.

With a screech, Beth hurled herself forward in the dimness to hammer frantically against the solid wood panelling, convinced that some devilish trap had closed upon her.

To her amazement and sobbing relief, the handle gave a rattle and the door swung slowly open once more.

Beth stumbled into the sunlight.

'What in God's name are you doing down there?' Esther was staring at her in astonishment.

'You locked me in,' Beth choked. 'You locked me in.'

'I didn't know you were down there. I saw the key in the door and thought I'd forgotten to remove it. What were you doing in my cellar?'

'You're growing mushrooms.'

'There's no law against it, is there? I like mushrooms. And since the mushroom-meadows have been destroyed there are few sites where they can be found.' She scowled. 'I had some idea of making an honest penny by selling them. Only Violet Pettifer's death scotched that. People would probably believe I was trying to poison them.'

'She didn't get hers from you?'

'Of course she didn't damned well get them from me.' Esther glared at her. 'Mine are proper mushrooms, look for yourself. Anyhow, what were you searching for?'

'I wondered what you kept in there,' said Beth lamely. 'You always jumped guiltily when anyone came this way, and you kept the door locked — '

'Against the thieving peasants,' said Esther starkly. 'And if I jumped it was hardly from guilt. What did you expect me to have in there? The proceeds of Kenlake House robbery?' She gave a great crack of laughter. 'I believe you did, at that.' She led the girl up the mossed steps from the cellar. 'Take care, Beth. People who pry are apt to regret it. As I told Reuben, turn a stone and you'll find maggots crawl out. The golden rule in this life, girl, is mind your own business. You do that.' She flicked a bright glance. 'And I'll mind mine.'

Slowly she walked across to the terrace and stood there watching while Beth started the Land-Rover.

'And find Reuben,' she called as her parting shot.

But Reuben was nowhere to be found. Back at the farm, Beth made for the oast-houses and the hop-picking machine, but neither was in operation and no one was there. A quick glance inside the great dim machinery-shed and a call up the ladder to the drying-floor of the kilns produced no results. Everywhere was silent.

'Where is everybody?' Beth asked Lucy, spotting her sister cycling along the drive on her way to the village. 'I can't find Reuben and I can't find Tom. Are they in the house?'

Lucy shook her head. 'There's an

emergency at Brownings. T.J.'s taken everyone available down there — some of the students, anyhow. Tom is around somewhere. I saw him saddling one of the horses. Gone to the beanfield, or to the packing-shed, I expect.'

'And Reuben?'

Lucy shrugged. 'No idea. The longer he keeps away from me, the better I like it.'

Neither the beanfield nor the packing-shed yielded up Tom or Reuben and in the orchards, too, Beth drew a similar blank.

Puzzled, she made her way back to the oasts, ran up the wooden steps to the press and looked around. The smell of hops was thick in the shimmering heat. But nobody was there. From the upper floor she could see across the yard and out towards the deserted hopfields. No one. Nothing. Only a white vapour-trail high in the blue sky.

Once more on the ground, she went for a second time over to the hop-picking shed. That, also, was quite empty, stifling under the hot sun. Even the lunch haversacks had gone. Possibly the machine had broken down again. But then — her hand poised on the doorframe as she glanced within — surely Reuben, at least, would be in there fixing things? She stared towards the far end of the shed before walking slowly forward.

Hop-bines were still dangling from the belt hooks, ready to be dragged into the vast hop-picking machine. But the metal guard at the front had been removed, unscrewed, and was standing on the floor. Some repair work was obviously in progress. On an impulse, she threw a couple of switches and the iron monster clanked into action, slowly pulling the nearest hop-bine into its mighty maw. Beth switched the current off again. The main working gear, then, was all right. Whatever was holding things up could be of a trivial nature only.

Perhaps Tom, and Reuben too, had gone with T.J.?

She bit her lip. It seemed unlikely. T.J. would have insisted that Tom stayed behind at the farm to dance attendance on the oasts and perform a hundred and one other jobs.

And Reuben?

She raised her eyes to the motionless belt with its load of waiting hop-bines. And went cold. He was there, hanging high from one of the belt hooks, just in front of the machine.

Her breath drew in on a painful rasp.

'No. Oh, *no*,' she whispered.

A well-leafed bine obscured most of his torso, but his face was inclined towards her, a lock of the black hair drooping over the sightless eyes. His mouth was open, the lips drawn back from the teeth as if in a snarl, and his fingers, thrusting bone-white between the large, dark leaves, were splayed like spokes. Very gently, his body rotated away from her as the hook above him shivered with dying vibrations from the now silent machinery. The small green hops about him trembled.

Earlier, she realised now, the heavy foliage must have hidden him from her sight, or her eyes, accustomed to the brightness outside, had failed to spot him in the shadows of the shed. Either way, she had missed him. Then she remembered that she herself had switched on the mechanism which had pulled him into view. Another few moments and he would have been dragged across the missing guard —

She took another step forward.

From the tail of her eye she caught a sudden flash of movement, a momentary impression of someone or something in green, coming swiftly at her. Then a blow took her hard on the back of her head and she went out like a shattered lamp.

11

Water was running somewhere to her right, a regular fall and plash against stone that made her think of the river Addot tumbling its boulder-strewn way along the reaches beyond Ashpool. The sun shone warm on her closed eyelids and the air was full of an overpowering smell of hops. A drowsy, drug-laden aroma which seemed to press upon her senses so that it was a wearisome effort to open her eyes. Above her was the sky, blue as cornflowers, with here and there a patch of curdled cloud, and, nearer at hand, hovering so close that his breath fanned her cheek, Tom's anxious face swam into view.

'Thank God!' he said fervently. 'Thank God that you're all right.' His arms tightened on her convulsively.

Turning her head, Beth found she was behind the shed which housed the hop-picking machine. She was lying on a

pile of debris from the stripped hop-
bines, a vast cushion of torn leaves and
husk and fragments of stem ejected from
an outlet in the wall above her. Pheasants
were pecking a few paces beyond her feet,
tame as hens.

Memory seeped back.

'How did I get out here?' she queried
slowly, feeling the pain lance through her
skull as she moved to look up at her
brother.

'I've no idea, I was hoping you could
tell me,' Tom replied. 'I've just ridden in.
What happened?' He was supporting her
shoulders and gently swabbing her head
with cold water. A great deal of this had
trickled down her neck and soaked her
blouse. In fact, from the state of her utter
saturation, Beth suspected that Tom had
panicked earlier and treated her to a
whole bucketful from the water stand-
pipe, which was still flowing, splashing a
glittering path on to the concrete below.
The grey dust that caked his riding-boots
was mottled with dark droplets.

Beth frowned, remembering. 'Someone
hit me. Inside the machine-shed.' She

pushed his hand away feebly. 'Put a sock in it, Tom, you're drenching me.' She pulled at the wet front of her blouse. 'That's enough. Turn off that tap.' She tried to struggle away from him and again a violent pain struck her between the eyes. For a moment the brilliant day heeled in splinters around her, then gradually righted itself.

Beth put both hands to her head. 'God,' she groaned.

'Are you all right?' asked Tom. 'You're not going to faint again, are you?' He favoured her with another generous half bucket of water.

'Tom!' Beth howled through the ice-cold cascade. 'I'm okay. Or I will be, if you quit the death-by-drowning routine.' She wiped her face with her hand. If she performed every action at a snail's pace, and if she kept her head still, she found that movement was bearable.

Tom helped her to her feet.

'Did you find me here?' she asked, when she was safely upright.

'Yes. Spread like Sleeping Beauty on that pile of leaves. Out cold. I thought you'd fainted.' He was looking at her doubtfully. 'Hadn't you better go and lie down?'

'No. Mother will fuss. Besides, I told you, I didn't faint. Someone gave me a belt over the ear. In there.' She went to nod her head towards the machine-shed and quickly changed her mind. She jabbed with a thumb instead.

'Who on earth would hit you?'

'I don't know, do I?' replied Beth crossly. 'I only caught a glimpse. Some-one in a hood and green protective clothing, I think.'

Tom was exploring her scalp with gentle fingers.

'You really have got a bump,' he said. 'Rather a nasty one, just here.' He pressed lightly.

'Ouch!'

'Sorry.' He flicked her a smile. 'But are you sure you didn't bang into the door-post?'

'How? Walking backwards?' suggested Beth acidly. She scowled. 'And I was inside. How do you account for having found me out here?'

'You might have tripped in the shed, somehow,' said Tom. 'Knocked your head on something and reeled outside. A blow to the skull can make a person do peculiar things. Even cause a lapse of memory.'

'I did not trip,' bit off Beth between clenched teeth. 'And my memory is fine . . . I went inside the shed to look for Reuben — '

'I was looking for him, too,' said Tom. 'It's about time he gave me a hand. It's chaos down at the packing-shed. The first boxes haven't been collected yet and T.J.'s walked off with most of the workers . . . And I'm spending the day galloping between orchard, shed and beanfield. Then there's this lot waiting for me.' He waved his hands at the sacks of hops which were standing by the elevator ready to go up to the drying-floor of the oasts. 'We'll be working here all night.'

But Beth did not appear to be listening. The whole horror of the day had come flooding back to her. Reuben! Of course. Reuben!

'Tom — ' She clutched his arm. 'Tom!

Reuben is in there, in the machine-shed. He's dead.'

Tom looked at her from the corner of his eyes. 'I've just been in there,' he said. 'There's no one in there. The shed's empty.'

Beth shook his arm. 'Then you didn't spot him. He's hanging from one of the hop-bine hooks, near the machine. And he's dead.'

Again Tom gave her a slanting, guarded look. 'You must have hit your head harder than we thought.' He stooped slightly to peer into her eyes. 'You look normal enough,' he murmured. 'But perhaps one can't always tell with concussion. Maybe the doctor should check you over.'

'Tom! I'm not hallucinating,' Beth insisted. 'Come with me. There's one sure way to settle this.' She towed him into the machine-shed and along to the hop-bine where she had seen Reuben hanging. 'There,' she said triumphantly.

But Reuben had gone.

All that was hanging from the hop-bine hook now was the hop-bine itself and Reuben's jacket, as if he had grown too hot and had draped it there while he worked.

Beth's eyes rounded in disbelief.

'Steady, comrade. It's just his jacket,' said Tom.

'I can see that,' replied Beth in irritation. 'I'm not blind. Neither am I daft. A few minutes ago Reuben was hanging there. And he was dead. He had a great wound at the side of his head and there was blood — ' Her voice trailed away. 'He wasn't even wearing a jacket, just his green-checked shirt. You *must* have seen him. He was here only a moment ago . . . ' A sudden thought occurred to her. 'What time is it?'

Wordlessly, Tom held his watch towards her. Beth eyed it in panic. Over an hour had passed since she had seen the dead man. She must have been unconscious for a whole hour. Was that possible? She fingered the lump on her head gingerly. Other than a slight headache and a curiously rough, parched sensation in her mouth, she felt fine. Certainly not concussed, nor half-witted.

She licked her dry lips. 'Tom. He was

here. Hanging.' Slowly, she traversed the shed. Apart from the pair of them, it was quite empty, either of the living or of the dead.

Outside, the hop-bines swayed from their hooks in the sunshine. No Reuben there, either. No Reuben anywhere they searched. And, to humour her, Tom helped her comb the whole area around and in the machine-shed and oast-houses.

'He's not here,' said Tom. 'In my opinion you're suffering from shock and Reuben is perfectly hale and hearty and probably still at Reads' mill.'

Beth raised her brows. 'Reads' mill?'

'He went there early this morning, to deliver a coil, or something, from T.J. He should have returned by now, though. Unless he's skived off somewhere. We've been flogging the workers rather hard lately and they're all getting a bit browned off.' His tone was rueful. 'Perhaps Read has slipped him a sizeable backhander to stay and do a more congenial job.' He grinned at her. 'Tell you what, we'll soon find out. I'll give Ingham a ring.' He went across to the small hut by the oasts which contained a telephone.

Archer Read answered the call.

'It's Lover Boy,' said Tom, his hand over the mouthpiece. He shot her a glance that glittered. 'Do you wish to speak to him yourself?'

Beth took the instrument from him.

'Archer? Sorry to trouble you at this time of day, but is Reuben there?'

'Hang on,' said Archer. 'I'll find out. He was working on one of our machines.'

A minute later his voice was again in her ear. 'Beth? Are you there?' When she acknowledged, he said: 'Yes, Reuben's here. He's still up to his elbows in grease. Do you need him?'

'No,' said Beth faintly. 'Archer — '

'Yes? Are you okay? You sound odd.'

'Are you positive Reuben is there?'

'Yes. Why? He's been here all morning. I understood T.J. had given his blessing — ' There was a pause and when Beth did not reply Archer went on: 'Sorry, Beth, to rush you, but if there's nothing else . . . ?'

'No. That's all. Thank you,' said Beth.

'Then I'll ring off. I've left the lad alone at the mill and he can't cope for long. Cheerio, sweet. See you.'

'Cheerio, Archer.' Beth put down the receiver. 'Did you hear all that?' she asked Tom.

He nodded. 'There doesn't seem to be much doubt, does there?'

Beth followed him from the stuffy hut.

'I saw him,' she whispered obstinately, under her breath. 'I saw him. Dead. I know I did. Am I going mad, or is everybody else?'

Tom turned to look at her, his eyes reflecting her image clear and minute under the bright sun. 'Beth, I must go. They need me at the packing-shed. Will you be all right?'

'Why not?' Her voice had an edge of bitterness.

He stood looking at her. A shadow chased across his face. 'Beth, go and rest. Everything will appear normal again once the shock of that blow has worn off.'

'You still don't believe that someone deliberately hit me, do you?'

He flashed her a grin that somehow did

not light his eyes. 'I'm keeping an open mind, shall we say? After all, who would want to harm you?' His finger traced lightly over her lips. 'You look tired, love.'

Beth jerked away from his caress.

'And I'll tell you something else, for good measure,' she gritted. 'This was not the only 'accident' this morning. Esther, too, had a nasty fall earlier, over a cliff by Dingly Dell.' Beth eyed him speculatively. 'She said that she was pushed.'

Tom's gaze flew back to hers. 'Do you believe her?'

Beth shrugged. 'She could be covering up her own stupidity, but — '

'Is she okay?'

'Fit as a flea and twice as rabid.'

'What happened?'

In a few succinct sentences Beth apprised him of the morning's dealings with Esther.

'Well,' said Tom, when she had finished, 'there doesn't seem much we can do there, unless Esther is willing to co-operate.' He threw her a quick, brittle smile. 'We'll discuss it later, Beth. I must go and show my face at the packing-shed again, or T.J. will be back and there'll be hell to pay.' His hand rested for a moment on her shoulder then ran lightly down the front of her soaking blouse. He could feel her heart beating against his palm. 'Go and change out of those wet things before you catch pneumonia.'

'In this heat?'

Beth watched him stride across the yard towards his tethered horse and swing himself to the saddle. His brittle smile flashed back at her.

'I don't want to run into T.J. I'll take the track through the hopfield.'

She moved slowly to stand at his stirrup.

For a second he sat looking down at her, his grey eyes hollow as husks. Then his hand hovered to touch her hair. 'Last night — ' he began. 'Forgive me ... ' With that he wheeled his horse and, curving wide, rode away from her through the green tunnel of the hanging bines.

Beth retraced her steps to the machine-shed and stood staring at the hooks where she had last seen Reuben. She was beginning to feel that her imagination must have been playing tricks. Perhaps she really had been dreaming. But the blow on her head had been no dream, her head still ached slightly. So did her arm. She glanced down at the inside crook of her elbow where a small puncture, like a mosquito-bite, showed an angry pink. She rubbed it listlessly as she moved across to the hop-picking machine.

The guard was still off and Beth leaned over to see why it had been removed. Presumably to give access to the stripping-blades, she thought. But they looked trim enough. No break in the metal. No buckling of the bars. There was a dry, dark smear along the edge of the outer blade. But it could have been anything. Oil. Paint. Even, she could imagine fancifully, blood. Carefully, she ran her finger along the mark and eyed the rusty flakes adhering to her skin with misgiving. It did indeed resemble dried blood. But it also resembled rusted iron. She bit her lip. Anyhow, even given that Reuben had been hanging from that hook — and, if so, where was he? — why should his blood be on that piece of metal? His body had never reached the machine.

Turning, Beth wandered across to the oasts and leaned against one of the upright wooden supports on the ground floor, staring out at the machine-shed opposite, her mind spinning in ever widening circles.

Firstly, Reuben wasn't dead: Archer had said Reuben wasn't dead. Reuben was with Archer . . . Her head went back against the post. But if Reuben *was* dead — If!

She knew he was dead, didn't she?

Beth came away from her support in a lunge. The thing was, where was he? She and Tom had given the whole area a thorough combing. But the farm was large; the district wooded and wild. There were numerous places where a body could be well-hidden. Yet — Beth frowned — that body would have to be transported. And who, in their right mind, would run the risk of removing it in broad daylight? Surely it would make more sense to hide it quickly, close to hand, before prying eyes noticed any unusual activity?

Her eyes ranged the yard, resting on the elevator outside and on the fuel-tank to one side which fed the burners. She examined the building where she was standing, noting the buff-yellow sack swaying from the centre of the ceiling to the ground below, its neck clamped beneath the hop-press on the drying-floor above. A limp sack which dangled like a shroud. She stared at it, her heart in her mouth. An enormous sack — taller than she was.

Beth stepped warily across and shook it. It was quite empty.

The sack continued to swing beside her, brushing to and fro in the dust of the floor. There was a dark stain there, too, on the concrete, just in front of her feet. A stain which was not yet dry. She stooped and swept her fingers across the damp mark and brought them away stickily smeared with red.

Like a sleepwalker, she headed towards the line of sacks which ranked the rear wall of the ground floor of the oast. They towered above her, all filled to bursting point with dried hops ready for collection by the breweries. Each one was swollen into a smooth tightness and was so rotund that her arms were not long enough to encircle more than half the girth. In her own mind she had no doubt, now, where Reuben's body had been stored. In one of these great sacks.

The question was, in which?

Picking up a knife from beside a ball of twine, Beth approached the ranked giants once more. There were at least three dozen of the monsters ranged in a double row.

For an instant she stood irresolute. She could imagine T.J.'s face if she split them open one by one only to find that she was wrong in her guesswork. Should she go for help? But to whom? To the police? Again, if she were wrong and the sacks had to be opened unnecessarily . . . Beth shuddered. To Tom, then? But Tom was on the other side of the farm, and she doubted if he would believe her. Her mind ticked off the possibilities. Archer? Archer who had insisted that Reuben was at the mill? Hardly.

And then Beth saw the wet patch which stained a small area near the bottom of one of the sacks.

She hesitated no longer.

A quick slash with the knife and the sack was disembowelled, spewing its contents on to the floor. A river of hops, running forward in a pungent wave across her feet, and, a heartbeat behind their graceful glide, the inverted body of Reuben thudding sickeningly to the ground, his head with the great gaping wound like a mouth towards her.

Beth gave a cry and started back, doubtful horror now stark reality. And found herself gripped and hurled round to confront Jordan Colley.

His eyes were on his dead brother.

For several seconds his stare remained fixed, as if he could hardly comprehend what he saw, then his attention switched to the girl still clutched brutally between his hands.

Ice ran down Beth's spine at the sight of his face. It was blazing with ill-contained fury, his eyes so hot and dangerous that their obsidian darkness glowed with an odd reddish light. If ever murder stared out of a man, it stared from Jordan Colley, then.

Beth drew in her breath, but before she could speak, or protest at his treatment of her, the knife had been twitched from her fingers and was at her throat. Her left arm was twisted agonisingly behind her back so that she could move only as her captor directed, and that only with pain.

'Jordan!' Beth gasped.

The knife caught at her neck in a savage little flick. She screamed, convinced that he was mad and was about to kill her.

'Shut that,' he said.

Beth shut.

'So you did for him,' Jordan growled. 'I said you would.'

'No. No,' whispered Beth. 'I never touched him. I found him.'

'You or yours. Where's the difference?'

'No,' said Beth again, desperate now. 'Jordan. You have it all wrong. No one here would kill your brother — ' Her eyes fell on the ghastly wound in the dead man's skull. But it appeared that a murder had been done, none the less. Her breathing came hard, as if she had been running. 'Phone the police, Jordan. Get the police here. Let them find out who's done this terrible thing. They'll investigate, find the killer — '

'The police!' Jordan spat the words. 'I can find my own killer. I know what's been going on here.'

'Then tell the police.'

'For what? So my brother's murderer can spend a few years in jail? No, my bint. An eye for an eye! A bloody tooth for a tooth. Starting with you.' The lust for vengeance glittered redly between his lids.

'Listen, Jordan,' begged Beth. 'Listen. We've always treated you fairly. I don't know what you're talking about. I don't know why Reuben was killed. I don't even know what your brother was mixed up in.'

For answer she found herself swung violently round like a ball on a chain and almost dashed against the wall. Jordan was raving, spittle gathering at the corner of his mouth and dropping to his chin. His mind was open to no arguments, his ears to no pleas.

'Then I'll show you,' he said venomously. 'Before I take you apart. We'll set a little trap for when the rats come back.'

Beth found herself being hustled at knife-point along the nettle-grown path that led to the rows of derelict hop-pickers' huts. No one went there now. The few itinerant workers were housed in caravans or had lodgings in the village. The crumbling buildings were used only to store old pieces of equipment which might one day come in useful — and never did — and the accumulated junk and jumble of the years, all rusting and mouldering undisturbed into quiet dust.

Jordan tore open the third door along, on the right-hand row, and flung her inside the hut.

At first Beth could see nothing. Then, as her eyes grew accustomed to the gloom, she saw the single room in which she was standing held a cobwebbed assortment of flaking iron bedsteads. A mattress, green with mould, was coiled in one corner and gave off a dank, musty, mouse-like odour.

'There!' said Jordan in triumph. He tossed aside several of the rusted frames and unclipped the front of a long metal bin to expose half a dozen well-filled sacks, which she recognised as the A-branded type from Ingham and Archer's mill. A design of a windmill graced the front of each. Flour-dust clung to their exteriors.

'They're sacks of stoneground flour from Reads' mill,' she said, puzzled. 'Full ones. What are they doing here? Is this what you wished to show me?'

'Very fond of sacks, you and yours,' he bit off savagely.

'Archer — ? You think Archer brought them here?'

'Don't play the innocent with me,' he snarled.

She watched him bend and slice the nearest sack from top to bottom with his knife. As she had expected, a stream of flour gushed out. Jordan attacked the next, and the next, with the same result. Then turned his knife on the remaining three sacks with an almost maniacal energy, slashing his blade into the bellying softness as if he were disembowelling his brother's killer.

Standing upright, he shook the tattered, empty sacks and raked at the piles of flour with his boots until the dust rose and swirled around the hut, chokingly.

'It's flour,' coughed Beth. 'Only flour. What's the matter with you? What has this to do with Reuben's death?'

'Where is it? Damn you, where is it?' His eyes gleamed at her redly from his dust-rimed face, like glowing coals in a bed of ash.

'What are you talking about?'

'The stuff from Kenlake House.'

'Are you mad?'

'Reuben said this is where they brought the goods. He knew. And he was going to try to cut himself in on the deal.' His eyes glittered. 'Reuben wouldn't have been killed because he found a few sacks of flour, damn you! Where is it?' He bent again to sift a hand through the white pile at his feet.

Abruptly Beth jerked to life, kicking the flour hard into his face in a swift, desperate action as she darted past him to the door.

She heard him bellow behind her, but paused only to slam the door on him and to heave the rotting water-butt beside it to the ground against his exit. The barrier would certainly never hold him, but it might serve to gain her a valuable extra second or two.

Running, she reached the overgrown path, but Jordan was already free, pounding at an angle across the rough ground to cut her off before she arrived at the farm buildings. Beth spun and ran in the opposite direction, away from the oasts where Jordan would soon be waiting, heading uphill towards the woods and the wide-flung outskirts of Reads' farm. There was a well-defined track, on the far side of the trees, which edged the Reads' place and entered Channings from the rear, through their own woodland and fruit-orchards. Somewhere there she might find Tom, or at least someone to help her.

Breathless, still running, though more slowly now, Beth gained the wood and hurled herself in under the trees. The greenness came down around her like a curtain.

Here it was peaceful, quiet. The only sounds, the murmuring animal, bird and insect life around her. And somewhere, not too distant, the rhythmic thudding of an axe. Beth leaned against a tree and caught her breath. There was no way, now, that Jordan could know where she was. She was safe. For the first time since she had confronted the demented man, she was able to stop and think clearly. And tiny incidents began to nip at her mind like summer midges.

Suddenly it seemed to her that the person she ought to see was Archer. She felt Archer had some explaining to do.

Weaving in and out of the trees, ducking under low branches, Beth at last found herself on the open track which snaked the higher downland. Circling to her left, she headed for Reads' windmill.

Archer himself came into view before she reached the outbuildings. He was standing beside a tree-stump in a freshly cleared section of ground just by the track, splitting short lengths of wood into wedges with a billhook.

He straightened his back at Beth's light footstep. If he found her dishevelled appearance disturbing he had little opportunity to say so, because she waded in without a greeting and with scant pause for breath.

'I don't know what you're playing at, Archer,' she gasped. 'But I do know that Reuben is dead and that you tried to pretend he was here. And now Jordan has gone stark, staring mad. He says the goods from the Kenlake House robbery were down at our farm, in your flour-sacks. He dragged me off to show me, but — ' She stopped. The quick intake of his breath had been noticeable.

'You found the flour-sacks?'

'So you did know they were there? What are sacks of flour doing in one of our hop-pickers' old huts?'

'Blast you, keep your voice down, or Ingham will hear you. He's around somewhere.'

'The police will hear me, also, when I

can get to a phone,' shouted Beth.

'Have you told anyone else?'

She shook her head. 'Jordan was after me. He's behaving like a raving lunatic.'

'Listen. You'll have to keep quiet — '

'I certainly will not. I'm going to tell my tale to the police, before Jordan kills someone. I don't know what's going on here, but I do know that I saw Reuben dead. He's down at the oast now. And you lied to me.' Her eyes glittered with tears. 'The police can sort it out. And I'll give them a good start.'

'Don't be a little fool,' snapped Archer. 'You can't tell the police anything.'

'Oh, can't I?' She took a step backwards. 'Just watch me.'

'Beth — ' He lunged towards her and she stared at him in horror, her eyes riveted on the billhook in his hand. A whole carillon of warning bells was ringing in her brain. He had lied about Reuben. And about how many other things? He really did mean to keep her quiet. Permanently.

Archer saw her face change, the

indignation becoming naked fear as she looked across at him. Too late, he realised what he was holding.

Forcing the paralysis from her legs, Beth whirled to flee, crossing the track at a sprint and flinging herself down the rough, flower-strewn slope the other side. She pelted madly over the field which lay behind Otley Manor, only to be brought up against an impregnable thorn hedge. Doubling back, she bridged the boundary ha-ha to her right at a flying leap to find herself on her knees on Ingham's beautifully barbered lawn. There was no sign of Archer.

Ingham himself was standing but a few paces away from her. He, too, was breathing heavily, as if he had been running.

'Well, now,' he said softly, 'what have we here? The little singing bird herself.' The colour drained from her face. She knelt hypnotised as he advanced on her. 'Oh, no, my dear, you're not opening that pretty mouth to the police. Ever.'

Before she could struggle to her feet, he

had pounced like a cat. One quick, savage blow to her jaw and she crumpled away from his fist into a defenceless huddle, her cheek pillowed against the velvet turf, her skirt raked high.

12

Beth opened her eyes to an odd greyish half-light that resembled neither dusk nor dawn; an eerie, filtered dimness heavy with a smell of chill and chalk, which reminded her of subterranean passages and old caves and smugglers' haunts carved from the limestone cliffs — or underground tombs. The air itself was tomb-like, unmoving, undisturbed by sound or breeze, and below her she could feel bare, cold rock. To her side, more rock, rough to her touch yet scoring under the scrape of her fingernails. Chalk?

Abruptly she raised herself to an elbow, feeling the hammerblows in her head. But panic killed the pain. Dragging herself into a sitting position she tried to look around her and a shower of small debris fell away from her feet with a loud rattle.

'Steady!' said a voice from somewhere nearby. The tone was gentle, but Beth reacted as if stung by a whip.

'Archer!'

For the first time she realised she was not alone.

There was the snap of a switch and a powerful lamp came on, lighting the ledge of broken boulders on which she was crouching and the chalk walls around her.

'Careful,' he said. 'There's a great deal of loose rock on the ground.'

He took a step towards her and she cowered back against the wall, drawing her feet up against her chest in a pathetic, silent huddle.

'Beth, I'm not going to hurt you . . . Beth!' It cut his heart to watch her shrink from him, to see her white, pinched, desperate face and the bruises on her arms and legs. Ingham had not been gentle. He saw her wince as she moved, turning away from him to hunch like a child with her face to the rock.

He rested a hand on her shoulder and felt her tremble.

'Beth, I'm going to put out the light in a minute, to save the battery. We don't know how long we'll be stuck in here and it's better to know we have power if we need it. Beth. Did you hear me?' When she did not answer he said quietly: 'Is anyone likely to miss you in the near future?'

He sensed rather than saw the faint negative shake of her head.

'Me, neither.' His tone was wry. 'But come someone will, eventually. We must just be patient and not panic. Someone will come. We know that Beth, are you listening?' Her stillness frightened him. He could feel her frozen fear through his hands. She seemed to have withdrawn beyond his reach. 'You must listen to me, Beth. Listen to me.' His arms tried to warm her against him.

'No!' she spat. 'No, Archer, never again.' She twisted to face him and he caught the shine of her eyes in the dimness. 'You and Ingham, both. I should have known.'

'You don't know; it's not the way you think.' Relief flooded through him as he understood the reason for her blank despair. He seated himself beside her. 'I have had nothing to do with Ingham's schemes. If I had, would I be here? You must believe that. Beth! I wanted to protect you.'

Beth glanced around her prison. 'So I see.' She rubbed her arm and croaked: 'Why are we here?'

'Can you think of a more efficient jail?' He gave a short laugh. 'I presume we've both been treading on Ingham's toes and he wants us out of his path for a while.'

'He's insane.' She turned to him fiercely. 'You knew! You knew about the goods from the robbery — that's what this is all about, isn't it? The stuff from Kenlake House?'

'Yes.' His eyes met hers levelly. 'I knew. But only afterwards. After the raid had been carried out. Ingham planned it, financed it, was going to dispose of the consignment. I found the stuff where he had stashed it, in the mill . . . '

Beth shivered and looked around her. 'Where are we?' she whispered.

'Little Tott. It's a small dene-hole, the other side of Hanged Man's Wood. This is the shaft.'

'Oh.' She stared upwards. She knew,

now. Little Tott, a shaft of some forty feet, with a low, curved chamber, or unfinished tunnel, opening from it. Many dene-holes were much more impressive, with deeper shafts leading to a series of bell-shaped chambers and horizontal passages. No one was really certain of their origins. They were to be found dotted about the chalklands of southern England and many theories were put forward to explain their existence — that they were marlpits or chalk-workings, or Neolithic silos used for storage, or ancient hiding-places for property or people in times of trouble. Occasionally the shafts bore notches for climbing.

Beth stood, her feet unsteady on the rough ground, still staring up.

'No — ' Archer gave a faint smile. 'We can't get out.'

He shone the light upwards, revealing where the carved foot-and-handholds ended two-thirds of the way down the chalk. He had already checked every available inch of their prison.

Watching her rub the inside of her arm, by her elbow, he said: 'That's how he kept you out.' Then, as he saw her glance of puzzlement, he enlarged: 'Your arm. It's how Ingham kept you unconscious while he brought you here. Some form of injection, I imagine. When I arrived down here you were sleeping like a baby.'

'So, why are you here?'

'Because I tumbled for the oldest trick in the book,' he said bitterly. 'You were staked out like a little Judas goat. I thought you'd fallen. You had pelted away from me as if you were some demented, wild creature and, when Ingham told me you'd gone over the edge of Little Tott, I saw no reason to disbelieve him. He was very distressed. He said a couple of our farm-workers had seen you fall and had rushed back to find help. Ingham had the Land-Rover waiting for me, with ropes and a first-aid kit, and he insisted on coming with me to give a hand. Others were supposed to be on the way with more ropes, a stretcher and the doctor. It all seemed highly organised.' He looked at her with grim eyes. 'Which it was. Only not how I imagined.' Catching at her fingers, he pulled her to sit beside him on the ledge. His left arm circled her shoulders.

'How did he persuade you to climb down here?' asked Beth.

'I didn't need any persuasion. Once I was sure you were at the bottom of the shaft, I was down here like a spider on a string.' He gave a faint grin. 'I was far too worried and much too impatient to wait for the help which was supposed to be coming. I tied the rope to the Land-Rover myself, very firmly . . . And you can guess the rest.' His foot kicked at the length of nylon cord which lay in an untidy coil on the ground.

He tightened his arm on her. 'Even when I saw the rope come flying down to join me, it was several minutes before I was able to comprehend that it had been released deliberately; that I'd lowered myself into a neat little trap and that there was no rescue of any kind in the offing. The only bright spot in the whole affair was that you were uninjured. Obviously, you hadn't fallen. Ingham must have carried you down here himself.'

'Like a sack of potatoes.' She threw him

a wisp of a smile. 'He went to a lot of trouble. At least that must prove he doesn't intend us any serious harm.'

'His day of reckoning is coming,' said Archer in a venomous tone.

Beth looked at him straight. 'Why did you lie to me about Reuben? Why did you say he was with you when he was already dead?'

'It was a simple mistake, Beth, that's all. No dire mystery, no terrible plot on my part. Reuben had been with us earlier in the morning, doing some machine repairs. T.J. had sent him up. When you phoned, I was busy. I couldn't see Reuben anywhere around, but I did spot Ingham, so I asked him if he knew where Reuben was and he said, still working on one of our machines. It seemed good enough to me.'

'But you tried to keep me quiet.'

Archer pulled a wry face. 'Yes. But not in quite the way you imagined.' His eyes were pleading. 'It was necessary to stop you talking, Beth. Believe me, it was necessary. You would have alerted Ingham and I wasn't ready. I told you, I discovered the Kenlake property in the mill, soon after the robbery. Ingham must have realised I was suspicious about those sacks, because he moved them — to your farm. Only, I'd already switched the contents. The real goods remained behind.'

'So that was why the sacks in the hop-pickers' hut contained nothing but flour?'

'That's right.'

Beth looked at him warily. 'If you were so goddamned innocent, I don't understand why Ingham hid the stuff in the mill in the first place. Surely he was chancing his luck? Common sense should have told him that you were bound to go ferreting around if he left it there.'

Archer gave her a twisted smile. 'Of course. But I think that was part of his plan. I was to be his safety measure. When the robbery went wrong and Rolfe was hurt, Ingham was afraid the police might be on to things too quickly. After all, the other villains must have told him that Rolfe was wandering the country-side; Rolfe might be caught, or squeal, or speak to someone. Ingham was all ready to switch the blame to me. My mill, my sacks, my brand and, no doubt, a perfect alibi for himself. I should have been left to talk my way out of a dicey situation as best I could.' His voice tautened. 'Only when he was certain that it was safe, and that Rolfe was already dead by the time Esther found him, did Ingham reclaim the sacks and move them out.'

Beth kept her eyes on him, knowing that Ingham would have been perfectly capable of shifting any blame on to his son. There was no love lost between them. Ingham would worry little about putting him behind bars for a very long time if it served to save his own skin.

Aware of her silence, Archer said anxiously: 'Surely the fact that I'm here now answers your doubts? I wasn't helping Ingham: I had nothing to do with the robbery.'

'Then why didn't you go to the police? When you discovered his cache, why didn't you inform them at once?'

For one moment he hesitated, then said: 'He is my father, Beth, whatever he's done. Would you have informed on him, in my place?'

It was the first time she had ever heard him voluntarily acknowledge Ingham's paternity.

Archer went on: 'I would have returned the goods to the rightful owners — eventually. But it wasn't as easy as all that. I had to find a way which would keep everyone in the clear. I also had to make certain Ingham caught no whiff of my plans because at the first inkling of any meddling he'd have moved the stuff out.'

'But it wasn't 'the stuff', was it?'

'No. But, if he had any cause to check on that, it was obvious where he'd look next. To me.'

Beth lifted her face. 'How long does he intend to keep us here?'

Archer shrugged. 'I've no idea what he has in mind. No one is going to miss me, are they?' His lips twisted. 'When will they start searching for you?'

'God knows. Everyone will believe I'm somewhere else — we don't exactly keep tabs on each other . . . ' She thought. 'Midnight, at a guess, unless Tom becomes worried sooner.'

Archer did not reply.

'I'm so damned cold, Archie,' she said, reverting unconsciously to the old nick-name, hated by Archer and tolerated by him only from her.

He wrapped her more closely to him, recognising suddenly how much he loved her. There were a great many things he had wanted in this life, but Beth Channing had always been one of them. Feeling her shiver in his arms he vowed silent vengeance for her sufferings. When he got out of here — When!

She was quiet for so long that he thought she must have fallen asleep. Then she stirred against him and said: 'There's still the question of Reuben, isn't there? If you didn't lie about his presence at the mill, Ingham did.'

In a low voice she went on to explain how she had found Reuben's body — and lost it again, only to uncover it at last in the sack of dried hops.

'It couldn't have been an accident?'

'Archer! He had a great hole in his skull. He could hardly have unhitched himself from the hop-bine hook and then tied himself neatly into a sack.'

'I know, I know,' he said soothingly. 'I merely wondered if he might have had an accident and someone had panicked. Tried to hide the body.'

'Why should they do that?'

He raised a shoulder. 'If that's not the case, then it's murder.'

'I believe Reuben was trying to blackmail someone — Esther hinted as much.'

'That figures.'

'And, Archer — ' Her voice was a thread. 'Jordan said his brother knew who'd put the goods from the Kenlake House robbery in that hop-pickers' hut. Only he couldn't have realised the sacks contained nothing but flour.' Her hand closed sharply on his arm. 'Do you believe Ingham could have killed Reuben?'

He rested his chin on her hair. 'Yes,' he said tiredly. 'If Reuben were threatening Ingham, then I think it's possible. Or had him killed. To keep him quiet. That would also explain Ingham's rough and ready treatment of you. Presumably, his plans for the disposal of the body had temporarily gone awry, so you had to be dealt with quickly, before you could start things humming.'

Beth sighed. 'And I had told you . . . Or so he must have thought. Maybe he heard me — I was shouting loudly enough. So exit Archer, also.' She gave a ragged little laugh. 'But how in God's name does he intend to keep us quiet?'

'Ingham? I don't know, Beth.'

'Surely he's not crazy enough to believe we'll say nothing? That we'll just let him go his own sweet way? He must know that when we get out of here, he's finished — unless his idea is to skip the country.'

Archer looked sceptical. He had an uneasy feeling that he had missed something important along the line.

Beth glanced up at him. 'Someone tried to kill Esther this morning — or so she says. By pushing her over a cliff.' Her voice was thoughtful. 'Perhaps someone believed Reuben had had more than a passing word in her ear, too.'

'Listen,' said Archer suddenly. He held

his head up in an attentive, ear-cocked fashion.

'What is it?' Beth stilled her breath. A faint wind-rushing sound came to her. No. Not wind. She tried again. Water. That was it. Running water.

But Archer was already on his feet, staring at the ground. He switched on the lamp. A dark stain was visible, spreading rapidly towards his shoes. His eyes travelled past the chalk wall of the shaft to the black tunnel-mouth of the small chamber beyond and he let out a soft oath.

'He's opened the bloody sluice.'

Beth stared at him without comprehension.

Archer was white.

'Christ! My bloody, so-called father has turned the bloody sluice.' Fear made him profane.

'The new Addot sluice, above Ashpool?' Beth sounded bewildered.

'Of course the new Addot sluice! Is there any other around here?' he bit out savagely.

'He couldn't,' said Beth, shaking her

head from side to side even as her eyes widened on the deepening inrush of water.

'What's that, then? A wet dream!' He was past her, peering in at the low curved chamber. Beth could see the water, like a smooth, wide cascade, gliding the length of the wall from some hidden fissure or weakness in the chalk above. The floor was already swirling ankle-deep.

Beth clung to her sanity. 'Ingham couldn't do it,' she cried. 'At least, not alone. That was one of the safety factors when the sluice was installed. Don't you remember? Mr Waterhouse and the committee insisted upon it. To prevent accidents . . . ' Her eyes were riveted on the rising water as she tried to convince herself it could not exist, that this was a nightmare. 'There are two wheels. They have to be synchronised, turned together — '

She broke off with a gasp as Archer grabbed her arm and towed her backwards, away from the entrance to the filling chamber. He cast a quick glance round and leaped up on the highest point of the chalk ledge, tugging her after him. It was not a true ledge, but a protuberance formed by boulders and debris and fallen chalk. The water was already lapping halfway up its side, another few minutes and it was level with their feet and rising fast.

'We're going to die in here, aren't we?' Beth whispered. 'There's no way out. Somehow, Ingham is going to convince everyone that there's been an accident . . . '

An accident!

So many accidents recently. So many deaths. Even through her fear her brain was coldly, logically, locking pieces of puzzle into place.

But how could this be made to look like an accident? Her teeth chattered against each other. Perhaps Ingham would merely return the sluice to its correct position when he was satisfied that there was sufficient water in the dene-hole to serve his purpose. If he just played dumb, who was to say he knew anything about it? The flooding would be attributed to vandalism, their deaths to the same cause. Ill-luck. No doubt some plausible reason for them to be exploring Little Tott at that hour would be brought to light. She would take a bet that somewhere above there was some convenient stump or tree craftily scored with the marks of a slipping rope!

The water was now above her ankles and cold.

'How long will the shaft take to fill?' she asked between chattering teeth. 'How long have we got?'

'Slowly, until level with the roof of the chamber, then quickly up the shaft — two or three hours, maybe slightly more.' He stared upwards. 'You can see where the water rose to during the last flooding, when they were using the new channel, before the sluice was put in.' He nodded to the watermark over a third of the distance up the shaft. The stain was clear in the light from the lamp.

He went on, half speaking to himself. 'There will be no flooded fields to alert anyone this time. This is normal river flow, not flood water, and the weakness above the dene-hole must be being fed from the new cut itself and is probably not enough to cause any significant drop in the level of the river proper.'

'Someone may notice the channel filling.'

'I doubt it. No one has cause to go there,' he said harshly. 'I always said that damned channel should have been filled in again and not kept as a handy drainage ditch.'

'Then, with the shaft flooded, we swim about, or tread water until we are exhausted and drown,' murmured Beth.

He flicked her a quick look. 'There's one chance,' he said slowly. 'Only a slight one and it depends upon us *not* getting exhausted . . . Do you see the notches? Just below the watermark? Once we reached those we could climb — if we still possessed enough stamina and if the cold didn't cripple us . . .'

'Any straw in a high wind,' said Beth, with a breaking laugh. She looked at him, her teeth still bared in a half-smile. 'I think we might manage that. You certainly could. And I used to be a stalwart water-baby. As Esther used to say, 'Not swift, but sturdy'.' She peered upwards.

'It won't be like swimming in a race,' he warned.

'Anyone who has once trained in our lakes should be able to take a little cold water in their stride,' she said stoically. 'And it's not mid-winter.' She folded her arms around him. 'At least it gives us hope and that alone makes me feel better.'

He said nothing to dampen her optimism; a week ago he might even have agreed with her. But she had been through a rough time recently. He wondered if the strength of her body would be able to match her will. And he doubted that he could help her.

'One thing . . . ' he said. 'You go first.'

And, in the end, it was that which kept her going. The thought that if she gave up, if she fell, she would undoubtedly take him with her. The horror of the black, swelling water in the twilit shaft, the claustrophobic atmosphere of the chalk walls pressing in around them, the small private terrors that caught at her from time to time, shudderingly, as floating, unseen obscenities touched her flesh, were as nothing compared with the nightmare climb towards the top.

With numb fingers, numb body and a numb brain, the easiest solution would have been to give up, to close her eyes and unclasp her hands and allow herself to fall backwards into the darkness and sweet oblivion. But one bright spark of willpower kept her clamped to the bitter stone; one unyielding part of her refused to be beaten and forced her limbs into a methodical, robot-like action which took her frozenly, unerringly, to the rim. She could hear nothing, see nothing. It was as if her ears and eyes had refused to function. She had no idea whether Archer were right behind her or whether he had long ago succumbed to the gaping grave.

Then her hands had caught the edge and with one last heave she tumbled over into sunlight.

Gasping, mindless, she lay prone, doing nothing, aware of nothing. The world had ceased to exist.

How long she remained there, motionless, she could not guess. Only gradually the sounds of life around her came back to her; the sawing of grasshoppers in the tall, dry grasses, the small chirrupings of birds, a light rustle of leaves and a sigh of grass, the tiny explosion as some ripe seedpod nearby released its burden.

And a rasping sound against her ear, almost an echo of her own breathing.

She was aware of a heaviness across her back, pinning her down. A bar of strength and warmth that was strangely comforting. Then she realised that Archer was lying beside her, sprawled, his face against her hair and one arm flung over her shoulders, holding her firm.

She opened her eyes.

Late afternoon, she guessed. Shadows thrown long from the westering sun. Insects droning through the dying heat. Jewelled fritillaries on the flowering mint. Scents of herbage and sounds of content.

The whole perfection of life in one shining droplet of time.

'Can you move?' Archer's voice was rough in her hair.

She nodded, twisting to stare into his eyes. 'But I don't want to.'

'Just a few yards,' he urged. 'Uphill. Into the sunshine.' He coughed, spitting water. 'Better for us. Dry out.'

She raised herself on one elbow.

Where they were lying was already in shade. Further up, the curve of the downs still dreamed in sunshine. A beckoning, glowing gold. Gold of light and gold of grass. Like honey poured over the hill.

Uncomplainingly she crawled and staggered after him, to collapse at his side on the warm, thyme-scented turf. Harebells and yellow potentilla gemmed the tawny rabbit-bitten chalkland under them. The sun scorched down. The air hung still.

Beth felt the glow of warmth returning to her flesh, the throb of life to her limbs. A sweet, vigorous sense of pure thanksgiving at being able to draw breath.

A wing of shadow crossed her face and she turned her head to find Archer's eyes staring down at her. They were vibrantly alive, glowing green, with something of the same feeling of exultation which filled her own body.

Archer smiled crookedly. Was this the sensation, he wondered, that swamped a soldier after some victorious battle? That same undeniable thrust of mood which sent him in to rape and ravage where he had already won the field? His prize. His relaxation. Deliverance after despair. Safety after danger. Calm after storm. The vindication of courage put to the acid test. The adrenalin so high that only total expenditure of himself could bring relief.

Bedraggled and bruised as she was, with the dark mark of Ingham's fist still showing along her jaw, she had never looked more desirable to him. The sun had returned the colour to her cheeks and the light to her eyes. She was warm and near and unconsciously inviting. And the boundary between love and lust stretched suddenly thin.

He knelt over her, his shadow covering her like a cloak, while the surge in his body became another kind of desperation. But she made no move to stop him. It was her smile, her eyes, her softness and open surrender that broke what little control he had left.

When he went down on her he felt her

arms reaching out to hold him and her body rising willingly, feverishly, to encircle his, until the insect hum around him was drowned beneath the roaring in his ears.

13

Archer opened his eyes and stared for several seconds at the clear curve of the sky above him. A sweep of his gaze across the heavens showed him a sun considerably lower in the west, the soft cloud on the horizon stained flamingo; the shadows longer. Despite the weariness in his body and the drugged contentment of his mind, he knew the moment had come for a reckoning which could not be avoided.

'Beth!' Rolling on to an elbow he pressed his lips to the corner of her mouth.

She lifted heavy lashes and gave him a drowsy smile.

'Time to go, my love,' he said. And swung to his feet to stand above her, looking down. His love. Now. And from now on.

Beth sat up reluctantly.

Archer put out his hand to pull her to her feet and stood with his body pressed to hers, feeling her warmth and the strong, steady beating of her heart. Her arms went about his neck.

He kissed her hard. Perhaps his old deep-rooted jealousy of her brother could be laid to rest at last, he thought sourly. Besides . . . Tom's star was fading fast.

Walking quickly, Archer led the way along the wing of the hill and did not pause until they came out upon one of the many tracks which meandered across the downland towards Otley Ash.

'This is where we part company,' he said.

Beth's eyes flew to his. 'Why? What have you in mind?'

He raised a sardonic eyebrow. 'I think that should be obvious.'

'You're going to tackle Ingham,' she stated flatly.

'I am indeed. And it will be no place for you . . . I want you to contact the police. Head for the village — then home. And have a hot bath.'

'I want to go with you. Ingham might be dangerous.'

'No. Do as I say.'

'He tried to kill you.'

'But not face to face, Beth. In the dene-hole. There is a difference. And that's just about his mark. Don't worry about me, I'm more than a match for Ingham.'

Beth was not so sure. Any way one looked at it, the trap with the water was an attempt at cold, calculated murder. And she remembered how Ingham had looked at her, face to face, with murder in his eyes. It was only his desire to use her as bait to catch Archer which had saved her then.

She plucked Archer by the arm. 'Are you sure Ingham will be alone? Someone must have been helping him — '

'Oh, yes, someone was helping him, all right,' agreed Archer. He stared at her for a long moment, his lips lifted in a smile that held the hint of a sneer.

Beth said hurriedly: 'I'll go for the police. Now. And some help. I'll find Tom . . . '

'You do that,' said Archer, the little sneering smile still on his face. 'You find Tom. That will really help me. Ask him if he needs any more flour.'

'Tom — ' Beth had a sudden mental flash of Tom in his room, chalk on the floor, chalk in his clothes. Chalk? Her breath snatched at her throat. Flour! It had been flour thick on his shirt and trousers. Tom had been carrying sacks of flour. But where? For whom?

But she knew the answer to that, as she now knew the answer to several other things which had been niggling at the back of her mind.

'Tom — ?' Her voice was a despairing thread.

'Of course it was Tom who was helping Ingham. All the way. It always was.' Archer's eyes were fierce on hers. 'Now — do you still wish to come with me!'

He swung round and strode towards the belt of woodland which stretched between them and the Manor. Beth watched him go, watched his blue shirt fade among the trees until her eyes were blurred with strain and she could see nothing but the swaying leaves. Then she turned her face downhill.

Archer had always been able to fend for

himself. But Tom? She had to find Tom and warn him. Give him a chance to get away. God, what a mess. And what were they going to do? Where could he go?

Yet of one thing she was sure. Whatever Tom had done, whatever he had been mixed up in, he would never have tried to harm her, never have been a party to that gruesome trap in the dene-hole. He had no time for Archer, but her he loved.

The path seemed to stretch out for ever beneath her flying feet.

Tom. Her heart wept within her. Why had he done it? Why had he become tangled up with Ingham and this Kenlake House business? Money? Probably. She knew how much he hated being on the farm these days. Perhaps this had been his way out. His ticket to freedom. With her? A stitch caught at her side like a dagger. Naturally with her. She knew how his mind worked.

Her pace faltered. She still could hardly take it in. Tom and Ingham. And, in Ingham's eyes, murder. Her brain began clicking in precision. How many murders? Reuben? Yes. She was certain of that, now.

And Violet? Georgie? Had he murdered them? Her calculations told her so. And Esther? Had he tried there, too? It all fitted into the same terrible pattern. Ingham was deadly dangerous.

And Archer was alone.

She gave a little sob and whirled to run up the hill after him.

★   ★   ★

Archer left the cover of the wood and made his way across the track and towards the stile in the hawthorn hedge that gave access to the mill.

It took but a moment to lift his shotgun from the wall and then he was outside again, swinging round the outbuildings and heading towards the Manor. He could see the pale gold of a barley-field lying like a stretch of water on his left, the ripe awns bowed as if in homage to the dipping sun. Mignonette in Ingham's border-walk scented the whole air.

Ingham himself, standing with his back towards him, was snipping away desultorily at dead flower-heads in a bed of roses.

Archer cat-footed across the grass.

'You won't be needing a wreath today, Ingham,' he said softly.

Ingham spun round as if shot.

'Archer!'

'The same.' Archer showed his teeth. 'Surprised? But, then, of course you should be.'

'What are you doing here?'

'Would you believe playing the Good Samaritan?' Archer brought the gun up under his arm.

'Watch where you're pointing that thing,' said Ingham irritably.

'No. *You* watch where I'm pointing it,' replied Archer. He gave a gentle smile in which mirth was notably lacking. 'And now, shouldn't you be on your way?'

'I don't know what you mean.'

'Oh, I think you do. And I suggest you speed things up a little. The police will be here at any moment.'

'You've told the police?'

'Beth will be contacting them just about now. So you've got about five minutes. To grab your wallet and run.' He stared at his father with mocking eyes.

'You were very clever, I'll grant you that, Ingham. The raid was planned meticulously. But then you knew Kenlake House like the back of your hand, you'd been there often enough, in the old days. All pals together, you and the Kenlakes.'

'Together with half the village.'

'But you are the one that matters, aren't you, Ingham? How much was it all worth? A million? Two?'

An unpleasant smile curved Ingham's lips. 'I've no doubt you're as well informed about that as about the rest of the affair.'

'Yes. You underestimated me.'

'I did, didn't I? I should have remembered your endearing little habit of keeping your ear to the ground and your nose in my business. However — ' Ingham's voice was satin-smooth. 'With Rolfe dead, and his associates out of the country it will be exceedingly difficult to prove I had anything to do with the Kenlake House robbery.'

'That's where you are wrong. With the proceeds still in sacks in the shed beside the mill, and Beth's evidence about the attack and attempted murder of us, it should be child's play.'

'Dear boy,' grinned Ingham, 'the goods went out of there the night after you showed such an interest in them. The heat was off; I no longer needed to hide behind you. Whatever you have been guarding so assiduously in your shed certainly isn't going to make your fortune. Nor is it going to delight the cockles of Al Begrar's heart. In fact, I should say the stuff is worth exactly its face value — the price of a few stones of wholewheat flour.'

'That's where you are again wrong,' said Archer, his tone silky. 'I switched contents before ever Tom collected those sacks.'

'You did what! . . . ' For the first time Ingham sounded shaken. 'You knew about Tom, then?'

'That wasn't hard to figure. Someone was obviously helping you and I knew it wasn't me.' Archer tilted the shotgun slightly. 'And now, shall we have done with this? The police must be on the road — '

'It will be my word against yours,' said Ingham. 'And you won't show up in too pure a light . . . You needn't think Beth will shop me, not with Tom's freedom at stake.'

'Like to bet?'

'You're a bloody fool!' spat Ingham, his eyes nailing his son. 'Do you realise that you're passing up a fortune? We'll go fifty-fifty, boy, and still be as rich as Croesus. A riotous old age for us both. What do you say?'

'Get lost!' The pitch of Archer's voice never altered, but underneath it was raw hatred. 'Five minutes, Ingham. You are my father, God help me — so I'll give you that. Five minutes. But it's all you are getting. And, at that, a damned sight more of a chance than you gave me.'

'And a grave error,' said Ingham softly. 'And one you might have cause to regret.' He turned away and began to walk towards the house. Archer grounded his gun.

'One thing, Archer — ' Ingham swung and paced quickly back. But now his hand held a small, deadly-looking hand-gun.

'Don't try anything, boy,' he said swiftly, halting a few strides from Archer. 'I can drop you in a second.' His weapon was trained on Archer's heart. 'And I'm not as squeamish as you are. Let the shotgun fall against that rosebush. Gently! . . . That's right. We don't want any accidents, do we? And now — step aside. Quickly!' He gestured with his gun. 'Walk towards the mill.'

Archer did as he was told. There was no choice.

'You're not so smart,' said Archer, when they came to a stop several minutes later. 'A bullet-hole will hardly look like an accident, however you wrap it up. But, then, you've made your fair share of mistakes.'

'Esther? Yes, I agree I messed that up — thanks to Beth Channing — but it won't be for long. I'll soon line up another neat little calamity for old Esther and, until then, if she chooses to say anything, doubtless people will believe she's as mad as her mother was.'

'Actually, I meant Reuben. And that must have been an even greater cock-up from your point of view.'

'Reuben. Ah, yes. But you can't really believe me capable of such inept work? No. That particular piece of bungling must be laid at Tom Channing's door.'

A stifled sound caught Archer's ear and he looked up to see Beth standing there, staring across at them. Her hands went out in a groping, blind gesture.

'Tom?' she whispered.

'Ah,' said Ingham. 'Beth. A gathering of the clans, I see. I've just had your brother here, gnashing his teeth . . . Come along, my dear. Stand over there, beside Archer.' He arced his gun gently and Beth moved like a sleepwalker to do as she was bidden.

Ingham smiled. 'That's the way. Good girl . . . Aren't we, then, to have the company of the redoubtable Constable Tate and his cohorts?' His glance flicked his son. 'It seems, Archer, that your plans, also, have run amok.'

Beth seemed unable to take her eyes from Ingham's face.

'*Tom* killed Reuben?'

'Tom should have killed Reuben,' corrected Ingham gently. 'But, regrettably, he faltered at the 'off'.' His teeth showed in a savage grin. 'A useful lad, your brother, but no backbone. And given to hysteria when the going gets rough. If he'd kept his head when Reuben first came to him, I doubt if the man's threats would have amounted to much: he was suspicious of certain activities, but little more. However, Tom's reactions must have convinced him he was on the right track, and a bit more probing and pressure set him up in business. Tom's nerve broke. And the Kenlake House affair was wide open. When Reuben connected Tom with me and the robbery he imagined he was on to a lucrative sideline. Blackmail. With me as the big wad — 'Venom entered his voice. 'But he slipped up there. I had no intention of being bled dry by some oily gyppo chancing his arm.'

'So you killed him,' choked Beth.

'With assistance, my dear.' Ingham's words came caustic. 'The funny thing was, Reuben had anticipated my reaction and provided his own insurance.'

'Esther!' said Archer softly.

'Indeed. Esther.' The line of the older man's mouth drew thin. 'I was informed by Reuben that he'd told her everything before he came to me and that she knew what to do if anything went wrong.' He grimaced. 'Whether his words were true or mere bluff I have no idea, but I couldn't afford to take any risks. Esther had to go.'

Beth lifted her lashes. 'So you killed her geese, and took her dog, expecting her to go after it . . . A fall from the cliff would have disposed of her nicely.'

'How well you put it!' sneered Ingham.

Beth stared at him. 'I wonder you didn't just toss me over, too. But then, of course, there was Tom, and he would never have accepted my death quietly.'

'You think of everything.' Ingham's lips lifted in a snarl. 'Tom was beginning to become a bind. While I went to deal with Esther, he was supposed to be fixing up a fatal accident for Reuben, with the machinery. All it needed was a quick clip

294

over the man's head with an iron bar while he was leaning over a tractor, or something. Accidents like that happen every day of the week. I relied on Tom's intelligence to make it convincing.' He gave a short laugh. 'It seems I relied on pure pap. When I returned he was gibbering like an idiot; he could no more kill Reuben than he could climb Everest. So that, too, fell on me.'

'You rigged Reuben's death to look like an accident on the hop-picking machine,' whispered Beth. She was breathing very quickly. 'You unbolted the guard, and the front bar, which you used to smash in his skull, and then you hitched him on to one of the hop-bine hooks, so he'd be dragged against the stripping-blades as soon as the machinery was started — after first replacing the bar you'd used to murder him.'

'Just as you say. Very ingenious, don't you think? Everyone would believe Reuben had been repairing the machine, had suffered some kind of blackout and had fallen — It was all set up, ready to go. Then I rushed back to the Manor to prepare my own alibi. After all, it might appear a trifle odd if I were seen wandering the Channing farm at the time of the accident: the oasts were hardly my province. All Tom had to do was throw the switch at the agreed moment and get the hell out of there. And he couldn't even do that properly.' Ingham's voice held acid.

'Because I came along,' said Beth. 'And spoiled things for you. I saw Reuben, hanging high and dry — and dead.'

'At least your brother had the presence of mind to give you a jolly good thump and lay you out.'

'So it was Tom who hit me?'

'It wasn't your halo slipping,' snapped Ingham.

'And then Tom panicked,' hazarded Beth.

'Yes. He didn't know what to do; whether to carry on with the plan, knowing you had seen Reuben hanging, or whether to cut his losses and hide the body. He plumped for the latter. Fortunately, he phoned me and I was able to organise things somewhat less crudely than he had intended. I also saw to it that you, my dear Beth, remained unconscious for rather longer than the bump on your head might have indicated. By the time you returned to the land of the living, Reuben was safely in his hop-poke, awaiting collection and disposal at my convenience, and I was back at the Manor, ready to swear he was alive and with me.' Ingham sighed. 'I was going to arrange for him to carry some goods to Connington — '

'And there'd have been a terrible crash on the quarry road. And fire . . . Very clever,' said Beth softly.

'But obviously not clever enough. I made no allowance for your sharp little nose still sniffing into things. Tom said he could keep you quiet, but I should have followed my instinct and rubbed you out in the beginning.'

'As it was, I ran straight into your arms,' said Beth. 'But I hope my removal to the dene-hole proved difficult. I hope you sweated blood to carry me down there.'

'It had its compensations,' retorted

Ingham. His gaze raked her from throat to thigh. 'Man-handling you was the least of my complaints. A pity I had to rid myself of you so soon, but you were the perfect bait for my son. I was aware it couldn't be long before he put two and two together and realised what I was up to — if he hadn't already done so — yet I knew he'd move heaven and earth to retaliate if anything happened to you. I knew you'd seen him and I guessed you'd told him about finding Reuben — and Archer would realise I'd deliberately lied about that. All in all, there were sufficient reasons for him to have more than a few doubts about me.'

'So, what have you lined up for us now?' asked Archer.

'Don't worry, I'll think of something,' replied Ingham. 'Maybe a fire in the mill. The consummation of flame.' He saw Beth's flash of apprehension. 'Rest easy, my dear, it will be quite painless. I'm not a fiend. You'll be well and truly out cold before I light the match, won't she, Archer?' He looked at his son. 'I believe grain burns like an inferno.' His head went back to stare at the sweeps of the windmill. 'Such a shame. But a suitable funeral pyre, I should imagine, for you and your — What shall I call her? Your sweetheart? That has such a charming, old-fashioned ring, don't you think? I hope, Archer, that you took full advantage of your tedious wait in the dene-hole — Such a waste if you did not.'

He saw his son's hands clench and said, the goading tone changing to one of cold menace: 'Don't try it, boy. That one puny swing you're thinking of taking at me would assuredly be your last.'

'You'll never pull this off,' said Archer. 'Not killing us. There have been too many accidents recently.'

'I do so agree,' said Ingham. 'But what is one to do? . . . When the hand is put to the plough, and all that — ' He stared thoughtfully at his son. 'Perhaps the fire in the mill should incorporate Reuben's body as well. He's over in that truck now, by courtesy of our friend Tom . . . Yes. You and Beth — and Reuben, too. Together. The devil of a disaster — '

'*You* are the devil,' said Beth.

His teeth showed white above the neatly pointed beard.

'Because I chose to kill our greedy and rapacious Reuben? The world should thank me.'

'But Reuben was not the start of it, was he?' said Beth dully. 'There was Violet. Poor, kind-hearted, garrulous Violet. It was Tom who told you about Violet's latest piece of gossip, wasn't it? . . . So you had to get rid of her.'

'Yes. As I said — your brother was useful, up to a point.'

'And it was Tom who told you about Georgie having seen the toadstools you gave her!' Her voice was breaking. She saw reason, now, for Tom's hollow despair, his blind need to blot out, in any way he could, the terrible things he had caused to be done. Violet, George . . . not by his hand, but on his conscience. Tom had known — or guessed — where to lay the blame for those 'accidents'.

'No,' Ingham was saying. 'That was your charming sister, Lucy, albeit unwittingly, at our party.'

'Christ!' swore Archer softly. 'What are

you? ... Reuben I can understand, maybe even old Esther, Beth and myself. But why, in God's name, Violet and little Georgie?'

'I know why,' said Beth bitterly. 'If Ingham possessed the goods from Kenlake House, then Violet was a danger to him. She told Tom and I that she'd seen the van and seen the men depart from it, but that they'd unloaded nothing. Do you understand, Archer? They had taken nothing with them. She was virtually telling us that the stuff was still there, in the van, waiting to be collected later. Even the direction it must have taken. Only I didn't realise it. And Tom shut me up ... Anyhow, you knew Violet — Mouth Almighty, Tom always called her. She would have to be prevented from broadcasting what she'd seen. So Ingham hit on the idea of taking her a gift — the basket of Death Caps. He remembered Violet had a weakness for mushrooms, he'd allowed her to pick them in his mushroom-meadows in previous years.' Beth sighed. 'Then Tom would deal with me — more subtly.'

301

'Oh, you're very smart,' said Ingham.

'But Georgie had seen the basketful of so-called mushrooms; Violet had told him they were a present — '

Archer broke in. 'A lot of people were aware they were a present. I'd been told that, myself, by someone or other.'

'Yes. But that wasn't the point. That didn't matter. After all, anyone could have made a mistake, picked Death Caps instead of mushrooms; there was sufficient loophole there not to condemn the donor, if exposed. Foolishness, but not crime. No. But Georgie had actually *seen* the toadstools, in their basket. So he was a danger. One small slip of the tongue and the police would be looking for a murderer.'

She frowned at Archer. 'Do you recall how everyone kept remarking how strange it was that Violet had made such a mistake? Remember, she loved mushrooms; she'd gathered them often. Even presented to her in a basket, as a gift, toadstools would have made her look twice: she wasn't stupid. But suppose she had been given a basket of *prepared* 'mushrooms' — Death Caps, picked and peeled and chosen for their very resemblance to the edible fungus? That would have been a different story. She'd have fried them and tucked in without another thought.' Her eyes sparked as they turned on the older man. 'And that's what happened, isn't it, Ingham? That's what you did?'

The muzzle of his gun swung slowly to cover her heart.

'Only,' she went on, again addressing Archer, 'Georgie had seen the offering; Georgie knew that the fungus had been already prepared, ready for cooking. Of course, the fact did not register very much and he never saw fit to mention it. Perhaps he never would have done so. But Ingham was afraid to take the chance. Ingham didn't want the police again tramping the village, asking questions, especially with the cache from Kenlake House still around.'

'Quite a little Sherlock, aren't you?' said Ingham.

Beth ignored him. 'So Ingham took Georgie to the water-tower; stunned him

303

somehow and drowned him. I knew Georgie would never have climbed that tower under his own steam. He suffered too badly from vertigo.'

'That I didn't know,' remarked Ingham.

Beth turned cold eyes on him. 'Killer!' she spat.

'Merely a matter of degree,' smiled Ingham. 'I've just had your brother here, weeping and wailing and wringing his hands because he'd suddenly discovered he'd opened the tap on his sweet sister.'

'*Tom* helped you to flood Little Tott?' croaked Beth, stunned.

'Who did you think attended to the second wheel on the sluice? Little Bo Peep? Efficient I may be, darling, but even I can't be in two places at once . . . Oh, I admit he didn't know you were there, but he was well aware of Archer's descent; he helped me to untie the rope. It was only when he found out he'd served you the same way that the hysterics started.' Ingham's tone was cruel. 'What did he imagine would happen? That I'd let you run shouting your findings across the countryside? If he was prepared to trust you to keep your mouth shut, I certainly was not.'

'You deliberately told him I was in that dene-hole when you judged it was too late to do anything about it; told him that he'd helped to flood it and drown me, didn't you?' husked Beth. 'I bet you enjoyed watching him break. But your gloating will have cost you your advantage. Tom will have gone to the police.'

'I doubt that. I doubt that very much. I don't think I have anything to fear from your brother. His nerve has gone and he isn't about to tangle with the law, especially as I pointed out that if the law seized him his family would suffer even more — he'd be on trial for murder. The killing of you and Archer — his sister and his one-time friend. As well as being an accessory to all the rest.' Ingham shook his head. 'Can you imagine what a heyday the press would have? Very messy.' He smiled. 'No, Tom will do what all weak men with a conscience do when faced with no way out — '

A soft swish accompanied his words, a moving whisper that was like the swing of a lash through the air or the downrush of a sword, and in the same split instant Ingham was falling. He hit the ground in a small explosion of dust.

Transfixed, Beth and Archer stared at the motionless figure sprawled at their feet, then up at Jordan Colley standing on the bank above them, his dark face suffused with hate.

The billhook imbedded in Ingham's skull said it all.

14

It was over. A week had passed since Beth and Archer had confronted Ingham outside the mill and Jordan Colley had taken his revenge. Even now a great deal of that evening remained a merciful blur to Beth.

From the moment Ingham had told her about Tom's part in the flooding of the dene-hole and his subsequent discovery that he had trapped his own sister, something had frozen solid inside her. She had known then that Tom was dead, known before ever they had come down from the hill to find a silent yard and a deserted oast, and Tom's body lying among the dried hops beyond the barricaded door of the kiln, from which had floated a single plume of yellow smoke.

Finding the shaft flooded and nothing to show that his victims had not drowned, her brother had returned to the farm, taken his shotgun, set the burner below the kiln at maximum to indicate the oast was being fired and thus discourage any early interruption, closed the door of the drying-floor behind him and blown his brains out.

Of Jordan Colley there had been no further sign. He had slipped away through the woods and was probably even now being sheltered somewhere far distant by relatives well-accustomed to outmanoeuvring the law.

The proceeds of the robbery had, of course, been removed by the police from the shed beside the mill and were, presumably, going through the process of being restored to a grateful Adnan Al Begrar. Archer had not come out of that part too well, but after exhaustive questioning he had been allowed to go. After all, as he muttered rather sullenly to Beth, the goods had eventually gone home to roost and it was doubtful whether the owners of Kenlake House would welcome any further publicity.

Beth remained stunned, frozen.

She did as she was told, went where she

was bidden, ate, drank and even slept as she was directed. Nothing, it seemed, impinged on her state of tranced acquiescence.

Archer looked at her now. She was dressed neatly, her skin was clear, her eyes steady. It was only when he caught and held her smoky-grey gaze that he sensed the hollowness within.

He touched her arm. 'Fetch your coat; we're off to see Esther.'

The large blank eyes turned to his. For the first time in days there came slight rebellion.

'I don't want to see Esther.' Somehow, sometime, somewhere, Esther was linked with pain.

'I need some more of her elderwood. Besides — ' His tone was grim, ' — I'd like a word with Esther, now everything's back to normal.'

'Normal?' Beth sounded bitter.

'You wish to stay here?'

Beth shook her head. 'No.' She didn't want that, either. She wanted to wave a wand, put back the clock, retreat to a time past . . .

But she had to go on.

And for the rest of her life she would wonder if things might have been different had she chosen that afternoon on the hillside, after their escape, to return to the farm and find Tom.

Archer was smiling at her. 'Esther will be pleased to see you; you saved her life. She'll probably shower you with gifts.'

'Like rocks!' The smile was a pale imitation of his own, but it was a smile.

Gently he took her hand. 'It's a lovely morning. Shall we walk?'

The mist of the early September dawn had gone, leaving the meadow-grass and the spiders' webs which covered it drenched in dew and shining like a green and silver sea beneath the sunlight. The hedges, too, were web-woven, spangled with glittering diamond drops and inter-twined with honeysuckle-bines on which the berries hung plump and red, with here and there a solitary dying bloom. Later it would be a fine hot day, but now the air was cool and polished and the first faint tang of autumn trembled on its breath.

Esther's gate was blocked with the familiar fruit-baskets, tossed down and waiting to be carried to the orchard. Either Paul Pace or Andy, guessed Beth, must already have made the deliveries that morning. She followed Archer round the untidy piles and then headed for the house.

On their right the elder-trees which gave the house its name were still in shadow, their parasol-shaped clusters of berries black and shining wetly with the morning dew and dripping sadly on to the seeding thistleheads below. But where the terrace stood in sunshine nasturtiums burned along the edges of the stones and exploded in flames of orange, red and gold across the wall.

Esther was inside.

'Come in,' she called, spotting Beth. 'Don't stand there on the doorstep.' Her eyes swept on to encompass Archer who had loomed behind the girl's shoulder. The old woman stabbed a bony fore-finger in his direction. 'And you. Come along in. I thought you'd be calling on me soon.'

'I came for some elderwood,' said Archer.

'Oh, I know why you came,' said Esther. 'Couldn't stay away, could you, lad?' She cackled gently to herself as she walked towards him.

Her fingers gripped his arm. For a few seconds she stood staring into his face, a tall, upright woman whose eyes were level with his own. Then she said: 'Was it hard to say goodbye to a fortune, Archer?'

'Middling hard,' laughed Archer. 'But there wasn't much else I could do, was there? I was relieved to see the back of the stuff.'

'I'll bet you were.' There was a mocking note in her voice. 'And of all those Adford policemen, I'll warrant.' She turned to move across to the table. 'I was just packing up some of my corn dollies; the rector wants a few for a friend.' She paused with her hand on an open cardboard-box and looked back at Archer over her shoulder. 'You wanted one as well, didn't you? You asked me to keep a nice one for Beth.'

Archer nodded. 'That's right. For luck.'

He pulled a slight face. 'And at the moment we need all the luck we can get.'

Esther groped in the box for several seconds, then held one of the articles towards him. 'That's an attractive one,' she said. She was smiling. In her hand was a corn dolly fashioned like a horn-of-plenty and tied with scarlet ribbons.

Archer shook his head. 'Not that one,' he said.

Beth glanced at him in surprise.

'I want the corn dolly I wove myself,' he said, in explanation. 'Do you remember, Esther? The one I made when I came to see you, a few days before the festival concert.' He peered into the box, shuffled the contents around, then glanced up at her sharply. 'It's not here, is it? A Kentish Lantern, tied with lavender ribbon — '

'That was your mistake.'

He frowned. 'I don't follow you.'

'You forgot the tradition, Archer — Lavender for the last stand of corn. And for that only. The death dolly . . . Left to rot till harvest comes again. The propitiation. Don't you recall how the rule of the ribbons runs? Shame on you. Red for the poppies in the uncut corn, blue for the skies of summer and sky-hued cornflowers, white for purity and green for the rebirth of the seed, while gold signifies Ceres, the corn-goddess herself — ' She gave one of her harsh cracks of laughter. 'That's what you were searching for in church on the night of the concert, wasn't it? Lavender ribbon? Only it wasn't there.' She felt his body tense beside her, like a runner's on the starting-block.

'What did you do with it?' he gritted.

'Removed the ribbon, of course,' said Esther, 'after you had gone. And replaced it with a more suitable colour. Red, green, blue, gold, what did it matter? You would hardly be likely to care — or so I felt.'

She watched him closely as he examined the boxful of corn dollies. He sorted the lantern-shaped ones into a neat pile, then picked up the nearest of those and began to shred it apart. The straw fell from his fingers on to the floor.

When he had destroyed the dolly he picked up another, and another, his fingers working ever more feverishly as he tore them, one by one, into pieces. Soon the floor was littered with fragments of broken straw and lengths of coloured ribbon.

Beth stared at him in amazement, protest on her lips.

'It's too late, Archer,' said Esther. 'It's gone. The emeralds aren't here.'

His hands stopped plucking at the corn dolly he held and his breath went out on a little hiss.

'So you knew all the time?'

Esther shook her head. 'Only recently. This morning, in fact.'

'How did you find out?' rasped Archer.

'What is all this?' put in Beth, coming to life at last. 'What are you both talking about? What emeralds? What corn dolly?'

Esther looked at him, raising her brows. 'Didn't you tell her, Archer, what you had done?'

'I would have — when the time was ripe.'

'Would you? Would you really?' She cackled and favoured Beth with a sharp wink. 'But we all have our little secrets, don't we, dear?'

Archer gave a twist of smile. 'Not from you, Esther, it seems. How did you discover what the corn dolly contained?'

'I was curious. I wondered why you wanted it. First for Melinda, then for Beth. Corn dollies didn't seem to be quite Melinda's scene, and Beth was as capable of making them as I was. And you didn't strike me as being sentimental, lad. So I decided to look a little closer at your particular effort.'

'Then how were you able to pick mine from the rest? You said you had already untied the ribbons — ' His voice was flat.

'I knew you'd made a Kentish Lantern and even without the tell-tale lavender bows I could recognise yours at a glance. You are left-handed, Archer. It was the only lantern where the design in the straw spiralled to the left — ' She slapped a bunch of cornstalks across his wrist. 'I pulled the dolly apart, and hey presto! A deadly green fortune in my hand.'

'Oh, you're too cute by half!' His face was suddenly harsh and frightening. 'Where are they?'

'The police have them,' replied Esther serenely. 'Mrs Mumford took them to the village for me this morning, just before you arrived. I'm expecting a visit from the law at any moment.'

There was a hot glimmer in his eyes, but all he said was: 'So. What are you going to do?'

Beth broke in, her tone terrified, shaking fingers clutching at his sleeve: 'Archer! Archer! Tell me, where did you get the emeralds? Where? You said you weren't involved with Ingham's robbery. You swore that. You said — '

Esther answered for him. 'He reached Rolfe, Ingham's man who was later found in the ditch, before I did. I think he knew the fellow.'

'Did you?' demanded Beth. 'Did you know Rolfe?'

'I'd met him once before,' said Archer indifferently. 'He was aware that I was Ingham's son, but I had no idea, then, what they were hatching.'

Beth swung to Esther, gabbling quickly: 'Then it doesn't matter, does it, that Archer took the emeralds? Archer wasn't part of the original robbery. He hadn't been a party to the plan. Rolfe was dead and Archer was . . . tempted. That was all. But the police have the emeralds now, everyone has their property back. So it doesn't matter, does it? What Archer did? The police will believe Rolfe hid them in the corn dolly. Or Ingham, or Tom . . . ' Her voice broke. She stared at Esther with panic-haunted eyes.

Esther ignored her, fixing her fierce golden gaze on Archer.

'One thing still puzzles me,' she said. 'Why did you put the stones in the corn dolly? You had them: you were home and dry.'

Archer gave another sour twist of smile. 'Not quite. I wasn't sure how things were going to turn out. Ingham had the remainder of the booty, but he and Tom might have been in the offing, searching for Rolfe, for the other members of the gang must have informed them of the slip-up with the dogs. And I wasn't too certain how much you'd seen — you had seen me, hadn't you? You nearly stepped on my tail — and if you mentioned that to the police, or to Ingham, then I was in right trouble if I had the emeralds on me . . . I came to you to see if you were going to say anything about my presence near there, but you didn't, not to me, not to the police — '

'It didn't seem to be any of my business,' said Esther. 'I thought you must have been with some girl . . . '

He laughed harshly. 'You would! I'm Ingham's son, aren't I? Anyway,' he went on, 'the corn dollies you were making that day gave me an idea. The emeralds could be left until called for, quite safely — or so I told myself.'

'Besides you didn't fancy all your eggs in one basket, did you?' murmured Esther. She threw a swift look sideways. 'At Otley Manor you had the rest of Ingham's loot to attend to, hadn't you? You had to discover where he'd stashed it and try to turn things to your advantage — '

'Archer was going to return the stolen goods to Kenlake House,' cried Beth. 'He would have done, given time.'

Esther's mouth curved mockingly. 'So

you really believe Archer here was going to emerge white as the driven snow? Hell, girl, you can't be as thick as that! Why do you think he kept the stuff hidden?'

'To save his father.'

'Pull the other one, dear — He intended to keep the cache for himself, when he had worked out a way.'

'You'll have difficulty proving that,' said Archer quietly.

Esther laughed. 'I don't have to prove a thing, lad. It's none of my business. And no doubt the police were satisfied with your explanation. You were lucky, Archer.' She glanced at him from under her lashes. 'And even luckier with the emeralds. The rest of the gang didn't realise that Rolfe had lifted the stones and, when the owners squealed about their loss, Ingham must have thought they were trying to pull some sharp insurance fiddle or, possibly, that Rolfe had taken the stones and hidden them earlier. God knows what acres of countryside the fellow had covered!' Her smile came crookedly. 'Yes, you were lucky, Archer. But then they always say the devil looks after his own . . . I suppose, when all seemed quiet, you thought it was safe to claim your prize?'

'You appear to be as well on the ball with that, as with everything else.' His voice sounded tired. Defeated.

'In some things,' said Esther, 'I had hoped I was wrong.'

There was the slam of a car door in the distance and their eyes flew to the windows through which they could see, at the end of the driveway, two men standing beside a car near the gate, where the baskets were hindering further mechanised progress.

Archer's eyes were like granite. 'Do you intend to tell the police? To hand me over?'

'I owe you nothing, Archer Read.'

'You owe me,' said Beth. 'Esther, you owe *me*.'

Esther gave her a long, considering look, then dipped her head.

'I trust you won't regret it,' she said softly. She indicated the French windows to Archer with a flick of her hand. 'Better if I don't have to explain your presence here now. Take the rear way, through the kitchen garden, and mind where you tread.' Her bright, orange-gold stare held fast to his retreating back as he went, light-footed, across the lawn.

She grabbed Beth's wrist when the girl made to follow him. 'Are you sure, Beth? . . . Like father, like son.'

'That's not true,' countered Beth.

'Rubbish! Archer will never be straight.'

'But he might be a little less crooked with me,' said Beth, flashing a hollow smile. 'And I need him.' Her head turned towards the garden again. 'You can make up some plausible tale to account for the emeralds in the corn dolly, can't you?'

'Oh, yes, I can make up some tale about the dolly,' said Esther dryly. 'Ingham's hardly in a position to protest.' She frowned. 'But at least I'll not have you go into things with your eyes shut. Archer won't tell you, so I must . . . '

With a savage twist of her fingers she spun the girl round to face her.

'Archer killed Rolfe.'

'No,' whispered Beth. 'No, I don't believe you.'

'Rolfe was alive when I came down the hill, when I saw Archer crossing the field below me. Until this morning, I wasn't sure — I thought I must have been mistaken, that my eyes were playing tricks, that I'd imagined the man's movements near the ditch. I'm growing old, my sight is maybe none too keen. So, when Archer dashed off like a scalded cat, I felt it had to be because he was up to some devilment of his own — obviously he didn't wish anyone to know he'd been in the area. And Rudd has a very pretty wife!' Esther sighed. 'Anyhow, what was the alternative? To suspect that Archer had forced the wounded man down in that water? It seemed improbable — Until I found the emeralds. Then I was sure. Archer has always been one with an eye to the main chance.'

'No . . . ' whispered Beth again.

Esther went on remorselessly. 'He gave himself away just now. Archer knew all about the robbery, all about Ingham's plans, about Tom's complicity about the goods being at Otley Manor — although he didn't know exactly where, even Rolfe couldn't tell him that — all about the raid going wrong and the wounded man heading for Ingham. This was no slow-blossoming suspicion of his father, Beth. He was well aware of all that when he came to me the day Rolfe was found. His actions admitted it. Doesn't it strike you that Archer knew altogether too much? And too soon! He *must* have spoken to Rolfe. Rolfe must have been alive when Archer reached him and, remember, Rolfe knew that Archer was Ingham's son. In his agony, is it too much to suppose that the dying man saw, in the boy, his salvation? He was on the last lap of his terrible journey, spent, and then, suddenly — the boss had sent his son!'

Beth's face was the colour of chalk. She swayed slightly, then caught herself up to stand rigid, her spine like a rod.

'Oh, yes, I'm sure,' said Esther. 'Now.' She nodded. 'Archer not only took the emeralds, but he murdered Rolfe, held him face down in the water of the ditch until he was dead, to prevent him talking to anyone else. It would have taken but a few seconds; the man was weak, dying. And I move slowly. Yes, Archer did it. The cuffs of his jacket were still damp more than an hour later when he arrived to pump me and stayed to weave the corn dolly.' She stared at Beth. 'If you can live with that ... My dear, it's up to you: there are other ways through this world.'

'Perhaps it should make a difference. But it doesn't. It doesn't. We've all suffered enough.' The soft voice held a trace of steel. 'You owe me, Esther!'

The two policemen were already climbing the terrace steps, there came the ring of heels on stone. Then the door-panels shivered under a sharp tattoo as the law made use of its muscle.

Without another word Beth turned, stepped into the back garden and headed after Archer.

Maybe she was right, thought Esther, watching her go: the village had suffered enough. 'For you, then, Beth,' she murmured. There was an odd expression in the marigold eyes. ' ... and perhaps for Tom.' She gave a small, close-lipped smile and, treading firmly over the broken straw which Archer had tossed down, opened the door on to a flood of sunlight.

THE END

We do hope that you have enjoyed
reading this large print book.

Did you know that all of our titles
are available for purchase?

We publish a wide range of high
quality large print books including:
Romances, Mysteries, Classics
General Fiction
Non Fiction and Westerns

Special interest titles available in
large print are:
The Little Oxford Dictionary
Music Book, Song Book
Hymn Book, Service Book

Also available from us courtesy of
Oxford University Press:
Young Readers' Dictionary
(large print edition)
Young Readers' Thesaurus
(large print edition)

For further information or a free
brochure, please contact us at:
Ulverscroft Large Print Books Ltd.,
The Green, Bradgate Road, Anstey,
Leicester, LE7 7FU, England.
Tel: (00 44) **0116 236 4325**
Fax: (00 44) **0116 234 0205**

THAT INFERNAL TRIANGLE

Mark Ashton

An aeroplane goes down in the notorious Bermuda Triangle and on board is an Englishman recently heavily insured. The suspicious insurance company calls in Dan Felsen, former RAF pilot turned private investigator. Dan soon runs into trouble, which makes him suspect the infernal triangle is being used as a front for a much more sinister reason for the disappearance. His search for clues leads him to the Bahamas, the Caribbean and into a hurricane before he resolves the mystery.

THE GUILTY WITNESSES

John Newton Chance

Jonathan Blake had become involved in finding out just who had stolen a precious statuette. A gang of amateurs had so clever a plot that they had attracted the attention of a group of international spies, who habitually used amateurs as guide dogs to secret places of treasure and other things. Then, of course, the amateurs were disposed of. Jonathan Blake found himself being shot at because the guide dogs had lost their way . . .

THIS SIDE OF HELL

Robert Charles

Corporal David Canning buried his best friend below the burning African sand. Then he was alone, with a bullet-sprayed ambulance containing five seriously injured men and one hysterical nurse in his care. He faced heat, dust, thirst and hunger; and somewhere in the area roamed almost two hundred blood-crazed tribesmen led by a white mercenary with his own desperate reasons for catching up with the sole survivors of the massacre. But Canning vowed that he would win through to safety.